PRAISE FOR
NANCY BOYARSKY'S
NICOLE GRAVES MYSTERIES

"full of page-by-page surprises"
–*Kirkus Reviews*

"…nail-biting adventure whose thralls are difficult to escape"
–*Foreword Reviews*

"a hold-onto-the-bar roller coaster of a mystery"
–*RT Book Reviews*

"Nicole Graves is the best fictional sleuth to come down the pike
since Sue Grafton's Kinsey Millhone."
–Laura Levine, author of the popular *Jaine Austen Mysteries*

"a charming and straight-shooting heroine"
–*Foreword Reviews*

"Well written, non-stop, can't-put-it-down suspense."
–Charles Rosenberg, bestselling author of *Death on a High Floor*

"Well developed characters in a rich English setting brings ample
twists throughout and all the way to the final pages."
–Eric Hoffer Award Gold Medal Winner 2018 for *The Swap*

THE

MOSCOW AFFAIR

a Nicole Graves mystery

THE

MOSCOW AFFAIR

a Nicole Graves mystery

NANCY BOYARSKY

Durham, NC

Published 2021, by Light Messages
www.lightmessages.com
Durham, NC 27713 USA
SAN: 920-9298

Paperback ISBN: 978-1-61153-381-1
Ebook ISBN: 978-1-61153-382-8
Library of Congress Control Number: 2021938194

For my wonderful and amazing granddaughters,
Anabelle and Lila

CHAPTER ONE

NICOLE HAD DECIDED THAT A BRISK WALK on her lunch hour would take her mind off her troubles. She'd strolled along the Miracle Mile, named by boosters who'd once held great hopes for this stretch of Wilshire Boulevard.

The sky was an impossible shade of blue—free of smog, not a cloud in sight. It was a typical April day in Los Angeles. A few minutes before 1:00, the temperature was a perfect seventy-two degrees with a light breeze.

The outing, even on this beautiful day, had failed to lift her spirits. Reinhardt, her fiancé, had been gone for eight months now. Where was he? What had happened to him? Was he even alive?

As Nicole entered her building, her phone rang. She stepped back outside to answer it.

"May I speak to Nicole Graves?" The man had an English accent, posh like Reinhardt's, but it was definitely not him. Her scalp tingled, and she felt a sudden chill. This was the call she'd been dreading, the fear that kept her up at night. Something had happened to Reinhardt, and they—whoever it was he worked for—were finally calling with the news.

"Hello?" the man said. "Are you there?

"Yes, sorry," she said. "This is Nicole."

"My name is Ian Davies, and I'm with the British government.

I need to speak to you. I wonder if there's somewhere we can talk in private. It's a matter of some importance."

The feeling of her tingling scalp was replaced by the feeling she was about to throw up. "Of course." She took in a deep gulp of air. "Why don't you come to my office? The address is—"

He cut her off. "I'm afraid that won't do. Our conversation must be completely private, not at your workplace where people know you. You're near the La Brea Tar Pits, yes?"

"It's five minutes away."

"Can you meet me at the entrance to the museum there? By the way, I'll have an associate with me. We'll find an unoccupied bench on the grounds where we can talk freely. I'm hoping we can meet today."

"Yes, all right." Her words came out in a croak.

"If you're free, I can be there in, say, half an hour."

Thirty minutes. How could she endure waiting that long? "Can you give me an idea of what this is about?"

"Not on the phone, I'm afraid. Can I count on you to be there?"

"Of course," she said. "How will I know you?"

"Don't worry about that. I'll recognize you from your photo in the news."

She winced. She hated the publicity some of her cases had generated and the fact that people she didn't know sometimes recognized her and wanted to ask questions she didn't want to answer. "All right. In thirty minutes, at 1:30."

After dropping her cell back in her purse, she took the elevator up to Colbert & Smith's new penthouse offices. Fighting back tears, she hurried through reception and went straight to her office, closed the door, and sat down at her desk. The red light on her phone was blinking. *Another new hire with a question,* she thought. They were always wanting her help with things they should be able to figure out themselves. Whoever it was would have to wait; she couldn't bother with voicemail now. Later, she would think of that message light and imagine how differently things would have turned out if she hadn't ignored it.

"Now, the waiting would be over," she told herself. She wouldn't have to worry about him anymore. Her eyes welled with tears, and she grabbed a tissue before checking her watch. Only five minutes had passed since Davies called. That meant she had to sit here with her terrible thoughts for another twenty minutes before she could leave to meet with him.

She couldn't help thinking of the events that had led to all her misery. First came Reinhardt's inexplicable disappearance. When she'd met him, he'd been a detective chief inspector for the London Metropolitan Police. Later, he'd taken another job that involved a lot of travel, usually with little or no notice. His absences became more frequent and lasted longer. The worst part was that he refused to tell her anything about his new position, what he did, or who he worked for. Nicole had assumed it was MI6, the U.K.'s equivalent of the CIA. These frequent, unpredictable disappearances had broken their relationship.

Then, he'd turned up in time to rescue her from the fallout of her last big case. For the first time, he admitted he was a "covert operative." He still refused to say which agency he worked for, just that he'd come to realize he wasn't cut out for the loneliness of the job and the rules that separated him from a normal life. That was when he'd proposed to Nicole. He was ready to leave the agency, find work in L.A., and settle down to start a family. He just needed a few weeks to debrief, hand over his cases, and finalize his resignation. As soon as he was free, he'd catch the next flight to L.A., and they could be together.

Weeks, then months, passed with no word except for a single hand-delivered note on her birthday, five months earlier. Nicole had done her best to find him. She was a private investigator, after all, equipped with the tools and tricks of the trade. She'd tracked down the florist in London who had his standing order for her weekly floral arrangements. The shop's manager refused to tell her anything. "Our client list is confidential, madam," was all she'd say.

Nicole tried a phone number Reinhardt had once given her for his personal assistant, but a recorded message told her the line was no longer in service. She'd even located the number for MI6. The woman who answered had politely explained that the line was reserved for anonymous reports of terrorism threats to the U.K. She suggested Nicole write an inquiry to a post office address in London. Nicole dutifully mailed one off. She didn't expect a response, nor did she receive one.

On top of this heartbreak, she got up every morning, dreading work. The job she'd once loved had taken a bad turn, and she only had herself to blame. News of her last big case had gone viral in the media in both the U.K. and the U.S., bringing Colbert & Smith Investigations a huge amount of publicity. As a result, the firm's business had grown three-fold. Jerry Stevens, her boss, had hired a raft of new investigators.

Many of the new clients were the superrich. Some were founders of successful Silicon Valley start-ups who'd sold their companies for hundreds of millions. A good number were connected with what L.A. calls "The Industry." They expected Colbert & Smith to do what disreputable Hollywood PIs did: discredit people who threatened their livelihood with lawsuits and accusations of wrongdoing. Detective agencies for these people were known to engage in illegal wiretapping, hire bogus witnesses willing to perjure themselves, and dig up dirt—much of it questionable—to discredit people accusing big stars, producers, and entertainment moguls of sexual misconduct. These practices had landed some PIs in jail, but Jerry didn't seem to care. He was starstruck, and his moral compass had pivoted 180 degrees from the straight-arrow guy he used to be.

Nicole refused to take on assignments she considered dodgy,

and this infuriated Jerry, who thought she was judging him, which—of course—she was. She was no longer his favorite investigator, even though she was the one who'd brought in his new clients. He got back at her by promoting her. She was now in charge of hiring and training the new staffers. He'd given her the title of vice president—silly in such a small organization—a raise, and new business cards, none of which she wanted. Now, instead of the challenge of digging into her own cases, she spent her time managing other investigators and handing out assignments she would have liked for herself. Six years before, she'd been the office manager at a large law firm. She'd become bored with the work and had left to take a job at Colbert & Smith doing background checks for the firm's cases. After a few years, she earned her PI license, and she loved the work. Now she was a glorified office manager again, and she was miserable.

She was pulled out of her spell by a fluttering sound at the window. It was the pigeon—at least she thought it was the same one—that landed on her window ledge most days around this time. She kept a bag of chips in her office drawer for him. She was reaching for it when she glanced at her watch. It was 1:27. She'd lost track of time feeling sorry for herself, and now she was going to be late meeting Ian Davies.

She grabbed her jacket and rushed out of the office without telling anyone where she was going or when she'd be back. As she boarded the elevator, she reminded herself that no one would care since she was basically in charge.

When she reached the street, she turned right and ran for the La Brea Tar Pits, arriving sweating and out of breath. Two men who'd been standing in front of the museum began walking purposefully toward her. Both were dressed in suits and ties, which made them stand out in this bastion of casual attire. One was older, perhaps in his late fifties. He was balding and his neck was slightly crooked, as if from an old injury, so his head tilted a bit to his left. He was carrying an attaché case and walked with a slight limp. The second man appeared to be in his mid-twenties. His fair hair was cut in a style that would have been considered conservative in the 1950s. As they got closer, Nicole took in his clenched jaw and unreadable expression.

They met in the path's center point. The older man offered his hand, and she reached out to shake it.

"Ms. Graves," he said, "I'm Ian Davies. It's a pleasure to meet you." He turned to the other man. "And this is my associate, Kevin Smith." Once again, hands were shaken before Davis said, "Walk with us. We'll find a place where we can sit and talk."

She met his eyes. "You've come to tell me something, haven't you?"

He looked puzzled. "I'm not sure I understand. The fact is I'm here in hope of enlisting your help. But let's find some privacy before I lay it out for you."

She stared at him, dumbfounded. This meeting wasn't at all what she'd expected. She asked herself a question she should have thought of when he first called. *Could this be some kind of a con?*

"Do you have ID that confirms you're with the British government?"

"Of course." He gave her a smile that said he wasn't offended by this request and stopped walking to take out his wallet. Flipping it open, he handed it over to her. The man's photo appeared on a card identifying him by name as a trade representative for the British Consulate in Los Angeles.

It seemed innocuous enough, but what on earth could a British trade representative possibly want from her that was so confidential? Without comment, she handed back his wallet.

They rounded a corner of the path then another. At last, he seemed satisfied they were far enough from other people.

"Here's an empty bench," he said. "We'll sit here." When they were seated, he observed, "You're cautious, as I'd expect you to

6

be. And I'm not here on behalf of the consulate. I'm acting as an intermediary. There was no time to go through normal channels. We were instructed by Her Majesty's Government to approach you and ask if you'd be willing to take on a short-term assignment. We understand you enjoy traveling abroad."

"Wait a minute!" She felt herself flush. "It's true I've been looking for a foreign tour, but how would you know that?"

He put up his hand, palm out, as if to stop her. "Please don't take offense. Our people check out anyone considered for an assignment. As a private investigator, you know something like 'enjoys foreign travel' would come up on any background search.

"Our government took note of your role in breaking up that human trafficking ring last year. Of course, they would have also done a deep background check before asking for your help. We're hoping you'll be willing to grant it. May I go on?"

Nicole was silent. A thought had struck her. Davies kept talking about the British government. No mention had been made of British intelligence or MI6, but she had the feeling they were the source of this request. What if Reinhardt was behind this? He might have recommended her for whatever this man was about to propose. If she agreed to it, would she see him? Beyond this possibility, her curiosity had been aroused.

"I'm listening," she finally said.

"I'm authorized to offer you a riverboat tour of Russia with one of the premier cruise lines. You'll have a deluxe cabin to yourself. It's a low-risk assignment that will take very little of your time. Otherwise, you'll be free to enjoy the tour."

"There must be more to it."

"You're right. You're to observe a group of your fellow passengers and report their activities back to a government representative."

She drew in a long breath. "This doesn't make sense. I mean, why me? I'm not even British. Why aren't they sending one of their own people who've been trained for this kind of thing?"

"I'm afraid that's not possible. A few days ago, the person chosen for this assignment became unavailable, and the agency had to find a replacement. As I mentioned, you came to their attention because of your involvement in that case last year. The government felt, at the time, that you might become useful in some capacity in the future. The decision was made that you'd be right for this role. Your nationality is one advantage. No one would suspect an American tourist to be working for the U.K. And—if you'll excuse what some might regard as a sexist remark—your attractive, demure appearance, as well as your skills with people, makes you perfect for this assignment.

"Please understand that we're not asking you to act as a covert agent. You're simply an observer who refrains from getting involved with these persons of interest. In essence, you're a tourist who's keeping her eyes and ears open. That's all. This is perfectly appropriate for someone who's a trained investigator."

"I'd like a little more information. Who am I supposed to keep my eyes on? And what have they done to attract the attention of British intelligence?"

"I want to be very clear," he said. "Her Majesty's Government, not intelligence, is asking for your assistance. To answer your question about why these people need to be observed," Davies went on, "someone in government decided they warrant observation, but I wasn't told why.

"Rest assured that you'll be perfectly safe. Our people will know if anything goes wrong and reach out to you. Not that there's any chance of this. If you do accept the assignment, you'll receive an email with your instructions, including the names and photos of the people you are to observe. You're to memorize this information and delete it before your trip. These individuals speak English and will be posing as tourists."

"You mean they're not tourists?"

"This is all I was told. Your job will be to discreetly observe them and report back to the agency handling this. Are you willing to take on the assignment, or do you want time to think about it? I'll need an answer soon. This is rather urgent, I'm afraid."

Nicole frowned. "I still need to know more about what I'm getting myself into. For example, you mentioned reporting my observations back to your people. How would I do that? Wouldn't it be risky? What if my targets become suspicious? They could hack into my phone and read my messages."

"The agency has that covered. You'll communicate these reports through a smart watch, which I'll give you. It will allow you to send a daily oral report. The watch's communication system won't be using the ship's unsecure internet connection. It communicates by satellite, like other electronic devices do for driving directions or tracing an individual's location. We've taken this to a new level and added text and voice functions. Your reports will be encrypted so no one other than our government will be able to understand them. If you become concerned about anything that happens on your tour, you can ask your contact to call you. This will also be done with the watch. Your travel documents are in an envelope, which I'll give you."

"How am I supposed to treat the people I'm spying on?"

"Just as you would any passengers you don't care to socialize with. Greet them if they greet you, but don't engage with them unless they approach you. Feel free to socialize with others on the ship. Just refrain from reaching out to the people on your list. Above all, it's vital that you keep this mission secret. Do not tell anyone, not even your closest friends or relations.

"And do not—under any circumstances—interfere with what these people are doing, no matter what it is. If you observe them engaging in suspicious or illegal activity, let us know immediately. Most importantly, do not give the Russian police any information. They are corrupt and untrustworthy. I can't emphasize that

9

enough. But as an American tourist, you're unlikely to have any contact with them. Now, what do you say?"

Nicole briefly considered what Davies had told her. She had a feeling this was probably not the benign assignment he'd described, but how dangerous could it be on a ship filled with tourists? What attracted her was the chance to get away from her unhappy situation at work. Instead, she'd be involved in a secret investigation. If the British government, which was more likely MI6, was unwilling to give any details, she'd enjoy the challenge of trying to figure them out herself. Added to this was the possibility of seeing Reinhardt. How could she refuse?

"I'll do it."

"Excellent. Now for a few formalities. In accepting this assignment, you cannot claim to represent the British government. Can I have your word on that?"

"Yes, of course."

"And you understand that you are not an employee of the British government. You have no authority to act for the government, and you are working voluntarily. Are we clear on that?"

"Yes."

Davies' gaze shifted to Smith, his young companion, who'd been sitting stonily on Nicole's other side. He gave a nod. Nicole decided he must have been brought along to witness this exchange, in case of complications later. She wondered briefly what those might be.

"Any more questions?" He gave a little laugh. "I'm sure you have many. I mean questions I might be able to answer."

"When do I leave?"

"You're booked on a 9:00 p.m. flight this Sunday."

"Seriously? Today's Friday. How can I possibly be ready by then? Don't I need to apply for a visa?"

"These arrangements are all taken care of. We have your visa;

your air travel is booked in first class with the return flight open. The cost of this trip is covered, of course, and there is a check to make up for the time you'll lose from work."

"I can take vacation time." Nicole couldn't help herself. As she thought about this trip, she was suddenly looking forward to it.

"That isn't necessary. We don't expect you to sacrifice your holiday hours when you're working for us."

"I have one question," she said. "Did Ronald Reinhardt recommend me for this job? Are you in touch with him?"

Davies paused a few seconds too long before responding. "Who?"

"Ronald Reinhardt. He works for one of the U.K.'s intelligence services."

He shook his head. "I'm sorry, but I've never heard of him. Remember, I work for the consulate, which is completely separate from intelligence."

As she watched him take a manila envelope out of his attaché case, she wondered once again if he was who he claimed to be. He did have an ID card that said he was with the consulate, but such things could be forged. If there was one thing she'd learned since becoming an investigator, it was to never take the word of someone you weren't sure you could trust. She'd do a background check on Davies as soon as she got back to her office.

He handed her the envelope. "Here are your travel documents, including your air tickets, tourist visa, and a brochure describing the ship's itinerary on Russian waterways from Moscow to St. Petersburg."

"I guess you were pretty sure I wouldn't say no."

Davies gave a smile. "I'm only the messenger. One more thing—the watch." He pulled a jeweler's box out of an inside suit pocket, opened the case, and took out a watch. It was larger than any Nicole would have chosen for herself but quite pretty, a simple design with a rose gold band and an iridescent, mother-of-pearl face. On the side, it had a knob used for setting the time and, above it, a tiny button. He showed her several sequences of pressing the knob and button in order to turn on the phone's voice and message functions.

She took it from him, removed her own watch, and put this one on. She held her arm up to admire it.

"Thank you," she said. "Do I get to keep it?"

"I'll have to check, but I doubt it. It's a sophisticated piece of equipment they engineered especially for this assignment. It has a translation function—English to Russian and Ukrainian. Oh, about the weather in Russia," he went on. "I'd advise you to bring rainboots, a heavy coat, and an umbrella. Moscow is a good bit colder than Los Angeles, and St. Petersburg is indeed chilly this time of year."

He picked up his attaché case and got up to leave. "It's been a pleasure meeting you, Ms. Graves. I wish you luck."

"Thanks." She reached out her hand, and he shook it. She didn't bother with shaking Kevin's hand or even saying goodbye. He was standing some distance away staring at the pool of tar bubbling a few feet from the path.

"I've got to tell my boss I'm taking vacation time and go home to pack," Nicole said. "This comes at a good time. I've been looking for a trip that would be a real adventure."

"As they say, 'Be careful what you wish for.'" He winked to indicate he was joking. "Be sure to memorize the list of passengers and their photos and delete them before you leave. Don't bring along anything related to this matter. Above all, do not tell anyone about it. You might say a friend had a ticket for this trip but fell ill. That would explain your sudden decision to take this cruise."

Back in her office, she once again noticed the blinking light on her phone, but she was too distracted by her interview with Davies to bother with it. She sat down at her computer and did a background check on him. Just as his card said, he was listed as a trade representative at the British Consulate in Los Angeles. His bio said he'd worked there for fifteen years. He seemed authentic, but as Nicole knew, just because he worked at the consulate didn't mean he wasn't also with British intelligence. It would make the perfect cover.

Next, she dumped the contents of the envelope onto her desk. She looked at the airline tickets—British Airways, first class, just as Davies had said. There was also a Russian tourist visa and a printout of an email confirming her reservation on the cruise. All of the documents bore her name. How did they know she was going to accept? She pictured them running her likely reactions through one of their behavioral algorithms. The notion made her smile. That kind of technology belonged in a James Bond movie. Then something else occurred to her: if Reinhardt had a hand in this assignment, he'd know she wouldn't be able to resist. Her heart skipped a beat at the thought of him.

She put the material back in the envelope and went to Jerry's office to tell him about her trip. He was on the phone, leaning back in his chair, his long legs resting on the windowsill behind the desk. She could see the beginnings of a bald spot in the back of his short, sandy hair and wondered, not for the first time, if he was aware of it. She could tell by his conciliatory tone that he was talking to someone he considered important. It was a good ten minutes before he turned and looked at her. He didn't smile, nor did she. He was still angry about her reaction to his recent decisions and "willingness to play the game," as he put it. And that was pretty much the size of it. Their easy friendship was damaged beyond repair.

"A friend of mine signed up for a riverboat cruise in Russia, and now she's had to cancel." Nicole kept her tone matter-of-fact. "She can't get a refund this close to departure, so she gave me her ticket. I'm leaving on Sunday. I'll be away until May 11."

"You're what?" He sounded incredulous, as if she'd just told him she was becoming a Scientologist or planning to live with an Indigenous tribe in the Amazon.

The phone rang again. Jerry glanced at the caller ID, and his face lit up, a sign that this was one of his new celebrity clients. By the flirtatious tone of his "Why, hello there," it was no doubt a woman. He put his hand over the receiver and gave Nicole a dismissive wave.

"Fine. Go," he said in a low voice before returning to his conversation.

She gathered her things from her office and left for home, happy to be relieved of any further discussion with Jerry. She really needed to find another job, but she wouldn't have to think about that for a while. This trip had come at just the right time.

CHAPTER TWO

THE FIRST-CLASS FLIGHT ON BRITISH AIRWAYS was pure pleasure. Nicole enjoyed the champagne and warmed cashews served on takeoff. Dinner consisted of Caesar salad, rare filet mignon, and spinach soufflé followed by a cheese course then a hot fudge sundae. Since it was a night flight, the lights were soon dimmed. Nicole didn't sleep well on airplanes, but she did nap off and on. An hour before landing, she was served the full English breakfast she'd ordered the night before. There was a four-hour layover at London's Heathrow, where she stretched her legs by window-shopping at the terminal's many designer shops. The connecting flight to Moscow was on Aeroflot, which had no first class. The service and comfort on this flight was way below the standard set by British Airways' first class. Boarding was delayed due to "mechanical difficulties," and they arrived in Moscow two hours late.

Domodedovo Airport was a huge modern complex with great expanses of windows and a confusing layout, but it did offer many of the amenities found at other big international airports. On the long walk to immigration control, Nicole noted signs pointing to showers and sleeping accommodations. She needed both but was blocked from the main terminal by a barrier attended by stern-faced, armed guards. They were there to make sure no one got into Russia without a passport and the proper visa.

Immigration control seemed to be a leftover from the old USSR, with its inefficiencies and red tape. Not only was the room hot and packed to capacity, but it also seemed to have no organized lines, just people jockeying for better positions and shoving their way past those ahead of them.

Another American tourist, a woman who seemed familiar with the process, advised Nicole to avoid waiting behind Asian travelers. "The Russians always stop them, search their luggage, and ask them a million questions. It can take hours!"

Since at least a third of the travelers appeared to be Asian, avoiding them was all but impossible. Nicole was relieved when she finally reached the second place in line. But the immigration officer made the woman ahead of her dump the contents of her purse on the counter. He carefully went through each item, stopping when he came across what looked like a hand-written receipt. He held it up to read it.

The woman and her traveling companion—a man who might have been her husband— stared at each other but remained silent, refusing to answer the official's question, which he repeated several times. From Nicole's standpoint, his English was clear enough, though a bit fractured. He was saying, "Where are the diamonds?" Finally, he left his station and brought back a supervisor who repeated the same question. The presumed diamond smugglers continued their silence while they were forced to empty their pockets. When no gems were found, the supervisor sent someone to track down their luggage. Time was passing, and Nicole wondered if she should switch lines, but this would mean she'd have to start all over again.

The couple's luggage was brought and searched. Still no diamonds, and the couple resolutely refused to speak. As fascinating as this was to watch, Nicole was agonizing about the time. It was close to 7:00, and she had yet to reclaim her luggage. The directions from the cruise line said the ship stopped boarding at 10:00 p.m., and the ride to the ship from the airport could be as long as three hours.

By the time two uniformed policemen arrived to take the couple away and Nicole finally left immigration control, two-and-a-half hours had passed since she'd disembarked. Whoever had arranged her itinerary had hired a driver to transport her from the airport to the cruise ship. She was exhausted by now, grateful to be able to sit and relax in the back of a comfortable limousine. It took yet another two hours to get to the ship. By now it was almost 11:00, and the gate at the wharf leading to the *Queen of the Volga* was closed and locked.

Nicole made several calls to the cruise line's emergency number. At last, the gate opened. A man in a snappy white uniform walked down to pick up her bags and motioned her to follow. The ship he led her to was not *Queen of the Volga* but the *Amadeus*. Nicole protested, but her guide gave a wave of annoyance and murmured, "Come!" He took her on a circuitous route through the Amadeus and across a gangplank to the ship anchored next to it. This pattern was repeated until they finally reached *Queen of the Volga*, anchored five vessels out from the dock. Even though this was only the start of tourist season, river cruise ships were out in great numbers, overwhelming the wharf's capacity. The man in white led her onto the ship and up two flights of stairs to the top deck. He opened the door to her cabin, put her luggage in the entryway closet, and handed her the keycard. He gave a brief bow—his only concession to civility—and left before she could put together a tip from the rubles she'd picked up at the airport.

She was too tired to take much notice of the suite except that it was unusually large and luxurious for a ship's cabin. Leaving her suitcases where they were, she went in search of the bed. She kicked off her shoes and climbed under the covers.

She tossed a while, unable to make herself comfortable.

Finally, she realized she was too tired and jetlagged to sleep. Surrendering to the inevitable, she turned on the bedside lamp and sat up to read *Little Dorrit*. This was at least the fifth time she'd read it. She never tired of Dickens' lampooning of nineteenth-century England's civil courts and the lawyers who made it their livelihood. *Little Dorrit* was a rare combination: a fascinating read and a cure for insomnia. At last she felt sleepy enough to put the book aside and turn out the light. She slept until a loud noise, perhaps the slamming of a door, woke her. She sat up, suddenly alert, her heart thumping as if from a nightmare she couldn't remember. She turned on the bedside lamp. It was 3:00 a.m. by her watch. Now she was wide awake and fairly certain she wouldn't be getting back to sleep anytime soon.

Nicole put on her coat and opened the sliding door that led to the suite's private deck. She hoped for some brisk night air and her first look at the Moskva River, but all she could see was the ship docked next to hers. She left her cabin and started down two flights of stairs that led to the main deck where she might have a better view. The deck's lighting had been dimmed for the night, but as she reached the bottom of the stairs, she had a clear view of three men standing by the ship's railing. They had their backs to her. One of them appeared drunk, and the other two seemed to be holding him up. But when he started to struggle, it was clear they'd been restraining him. He said something she couldn't understand; perhaps it was in Russian. His voice grew louder as the other two lifted him over the railing and pushed him. He screamed as he fell into the water, and there was a loud splash. The men turned in Nicole's direction. She froze for the briefest moment before scurrying to duck under a nearby lifeboat, one of several suspended upside down along the deck's perimeter.

She was stunned, not just by the violent act she'd witnessed but by the fact that she recognized the two who'd thrown the third overboard. They were two of her targets, people whose photos had been emailed to her.

They started running toward her. Had they spotted her? In the darkness under the lifeboat, she could hardly breathe. But they passed her by and took the stairwell to a lower level. Once they were gone, she crossed to the other side of the deck, sticking to the shadows. She almost cried out when she brushed against someone walking in the opposite direction. Thoroughly spooked, she ran up the stairs to her cabin.

After locking her door, she leaned against it in a state of shock. Her heart was still racing, and she couldn't stop picturing the man being pushed over the rail. She thought of the person she'd passed. He or she must have also seen what had happened. Who could it have been?

Her thoughts were flying in all directions. She slowed her breathing, trying to calm herself. The man who'd been thrown into the water might still be alive. She could alert rescuers. If they acted quickly, they might be able to save him. Then she remembered the British consul's admonition to stay out of her targets' business. But surely they didn't mean a situation like this when someone's life was at stake. She couldn't just stand by and let the man drown if there was any possibility of saving him.

The ship was silent. Was it possible no one besides her, the man's assailants, and the unknown stranger had heard the cry that rang out when he was pushed off the ship? She decided to call the ship's night manager. Hopefully, he'd know what to do.

Before she could pick up the phone, she heard shouting below. She looked around for her coat before realizing she was still wearing it. By the time she got to the main deck, a crowd was gathering. The others must have heard the man's cry and rushed out of their cabins, men and women in their robes and slippers, a few shivering in pajamas and bare feet. Among them were some whose names and photos Davies had given her. One of them, Mary Haworth, was leaning over the railing. She looked like a

Midwestern suburban housewife in a pink chenille robe and pink bunny slippers with curlers in her hair.

As Nicole glanced around, she spotted one of the pair who'd thrown the other man overboard. This one's name, she now recalled, was David Wynn. His accomplice wasn't in sight. Wynn was standing some distance from Mary. They didn't exchange greetings or acknowledge each other. Wynn was tall and thin with a dour expression on his long face. Leaning heavily on a walker, he appeared to be very ill, dying perhaps. Yet, less than a half hour before, Nicole had seen him help throw a solidly built man—kicking and fighting—over the ship's railing.

Just then, a third person Nicole recognized climbed down from the level where Nicole's cabin was located. Tyler Brandt, in his early to mid-twenties, appeared dressed to emphasize his role as a representative of youth culture. His baseball cap faced backward. He was dressed in a white, V-neck T-shirt and sweatpants. His feet were bare. These three illustrated something Nicole hadn't noticed before. The people she was supposed to observe were so diverse in age and personal style, it was hard to imagine them interacting, much less working as a team. Maybe that was why they'd been chosen.

The passengers—from the size of the crowd, practically everyone on board was here— were pressed against the deck's railing, staring down at the water. From the chatter, Nicole gathered these people knew someone had gone overboard. She pushed her way to the rail so she could see for herself. He wasn't visible at the surface of the dark water. Perhaps he was under the ship or another one anchored nearby.

Three crew members wearing diving gear and scuba diving cylinders pushed their way through the crowd, climbed over the rail, and descended the ladder fastened to the side of the ship. The night was freezing, and Nicole could imagine how cold the water must be. The men splashed into it and dove under the surface, looking for the victim. She wondered how long they had before he was beyond saving. Perhaps it was already too late. Once again, the grim spectacle of the man being thrown overboard replayed in her head.

The spectators waited silently, watching for the rescue crew to reappear. It was a good ten minutes before the two swam to the surface, hauling what looked like a lifeless body. They lifted him up the ladder and laid him on the deck as one of the men pulled off his breathing gear and prepared to begin CPR.

Nicole had shoved her way through the crowd so she could get a closer look. She was stunned when she saw that the victim's face was familiar. He was another of her assigned targets. His name, she recalled, was Derek Swan, a former professional ball player. Now, at middle age, his muscles had given way to fat. The two rescuers who weren't engaged in CPR were shouting in Russian, shaking their fists at the crowd and waving them back. Few, if any, understood their words, but it was clear that they were being told to step back from the victim and the man trying to save him.

Sirens could be heard drawing closer. Moments later, an ambulance and three police cars pulled up to the wharf. Orders were shouted over bullhorns, and lights went on in the ships anchored between *Queen of the Volga* and the dock. The ships unlocked their gates to allow police and medics to pass through. Passengers of those ships hurried out of their cabins to see what the fuss was about.

It took several minutes for Russian paramedics and cops to reach the ship. They were led by a short, barrel-chested man in a trench coat who was clearly in charge. After consulting with the captain—who'd just appeared on deck—the man shouted orders at the uniformed police officers. Some headed for the spot where the man had gone overboard; others went to question the rescue team and view the body.

The chief detective, if that's what he was, turned to the

passengers and addressed them in heavily accented English, shouting for them to be quiet so he could be heard. His accent— which might have been amusing if delivered by a comedian— sounded menacing, or perhaps it was his tone.

"I am Colonel Vladislav Kolkov of Moscow Police," he boomed. "Go to your cabins. Wait for police to question you. We need to know if someone saw this man killed."

A murmur went through the crowd. Was he saying the man was murdered? Or was this a misstatement because of his imperfect command of English? No one moved. Kolkov shouted again, this time louder.

"Do as I say, or we arrest you for police obstructing."

With that, Nicole and her fellow passengers returned to their cabins. Now sleep was completely out of the question. Nicole got out her book and tried to read, but even that was impossible. In her agitation, she felt anger bubbling up. She'd been stupid to accept this assignment. At the time, she'd suspected Ian Davies was being less than truthful when he'd said it would be easy. She should have turned him down, but the idea that she might see Reinhardt again had blinded her to any peril she might face. Now it was clear that the people she was spying on were dangerous— killers, to be precise. It made her realize that Reinhardt would never have suggested her for a job like this. He would have known how risky it was and wouldn't want her involved. But her biggest mistake had been to imagine there was any chance she'd meet up with him in Moscow.

Glancing at her watch, she remembered why she was here and what was expected of her. She had to report the murder to her contact. She went into the bathroom, and after turning on the light, she flipped on the fan to provide background noise. Then, she followed the instructions for the call feature of her watch, pulling out the knob on its side while pushing the smaller button next to it. With her face close to the watch, she spoke softly, explaining what had happened, the names of the men involved, and the identity of the victim. She pushed the tiny button again, and the face of the watch flashed twice, which meant the message had been received.

She walked back into the entry hall and, after taking her suitcases off the luggage rack, rolled them into the sitting room. There, she stopped and looked around, taking note of her cabin for the first time. The sitting room was spacious, perhaps ten feet by fourteen. The color scheme was white and gold with chrome and black accents. The most noticeable feature was a huge, wall-mounted TV. Two easy chairs sat on either side of a gray velvet couch. Behind the couch was a round, glass dining table with seating for two. The outer wall of the cabin, which was covered with drapes, ran the length of the room. Pulling it aside, she saw that the viewing deck she'd looked at earlier was much bigger than she'd realized. It was furnished with two deck chairs and a chaise lounge.

She wondered how much this suite was costing the British government and why MI6, or whoever was in charge of this investigation, thought it was necessary. Perhaps it was the only space left since—according to Davies—they had only a few days to prepare for her arrival. But logic told her they must have had a cabin reserved for whoever she replaced, the spy who, as he said, had become unavailable. Was that story even true? Nicole was beginning to doubt what Davies had told her.

She continued into the bedroom, which featured another, equally large TV and the king-sized bed where she'd spent too brief a time sleeping. She lifted her bags onto the bed then couldn't resist the urge to explore the rest of the cabin. The bathroom, done in white marble and black tile, had a full-sized bathtub and a separate shower as well as two sinks. Next to it was a small walk-in closet. On the other side of the bed was an alcove with a vanity table fitted with a makeup mirror.

She unpacked her things, using less than a third of the closet's hanger rack and drawer space. Back in the sitting room, she found a credenza with a built-in refrigerator, which was too big to be called a minibar. Along with several bottles of wine, it held soft drinks, mixed cocktails, and candy bars. This left plenty of room for other items in the unlikely event she decided to go grocery shopping. Next to the refrigerator was a wet bar. An espresso machine sat on the counter. She got a china cup and saucer from a glass-fronted cupboard above the bar and pressed a button on the espresso machine to brew an Americano. While she waited, she noticed an assortment of hard liquors sitting at the opposite end of the counter.

When her Americano was ready, she settled on one of the chairs in front of the TV and turned it on. She flipped through the channels, but the only show on the air with English subtitles was *RT News*, a propaganda arm of the Kremlin. The story of the day was a civil disturbance in New York, which *RT* portrayed as a race riot. She'd read about it in a British newspaper she'd bought at Heathrow and knew it was no such thing. She turned the set off and went into the bedroom to continue reading her book.

The ship was quiet, and time passed slowly. Every ten minutes or so, the murder would replay in her head, the scene so disturbing that she had to get up and pace around, wondering about the crime she'd just witnessed. Why would two people in the group she was following want to kill Swan, who was one of their associates? Perhaps they thought he'd betrayed them in some way. Maybe he was scheming to get more than his share of the loot they were after. Or they might have suspected him of being a cop who'd infiltrated the gang.

Finally, after waiting more than two hours for the police to show up, she decided to go to the dining room. She was hungry, and the breakfast buffet would be open by now. Colonel Kolkov hadn't said how long they were to remain in their cabins. For all she knew, the police had already talked to enough people and left. Nicole made her way to the dining room and placed an order at the omelet bar. She found a tray and picked up a cup of coffee, a few slices of bacon, and a Danish pastry. The dining room was empty except for a couple eating in a far corner. Nicole found a small table with a view of the water and sat, waiting for the chef to call her number when her omelet was ready.

She jumped when a voice behind her said, "Why you leave cabin, Miss Graves?"

She swiveled her chair around to see Colonel Kolkov. "I didn't know how long you expected us to wait. I was hungry, so I came down here for breakfast."

"My order was stay until questioned," he said. "You come." She glanced over at the chef, who was flipping her omelet. He gave her and Kolkov a quick glance then looked away. The detective led her back to her cabin, where he gestured at the door and said, "Open." He spoke in a growl, clearly annoyed at having to track her down.

Kolkov wasn't a big man, but his aura took up a lot of space. Although his chest was expansive, he was barely taller than Nicole. Most notable were his amber eyes, which were both piercing and all knowing. He had a broad face, prominent cheekbones, and heavy eyebrows. She wasn't easily intimidated, but this little man, with his puffed-up sense of authority, made her uneasy. Perhaps it was the murder she'd witnessed and her directive not to tell the police about anything her targets did.

More likely it was what she'd read about the Russian police. She followed the news and hadn't needed Davies' warning about law enforcement in Russia. The reputation of Moscow's police would make anyone wary of attracting their attention. Many of them were corrupt. While they'd take a report when a tourist was robbed, they were more likely to throw it away than investigate. On cases involving their own citizens, they were known to disregard established police regulations, as well as ignore international laws safeguarding human rights. They jailed people without charging them, only to slap them with serious charges later. These might include murder, espionage, or treason. They refused prisoners access to lawyers. They were known to extract confessions through torture. And most chilling of all, the conviction rate in Russian courts was 99 percent, a figure that had stuck in Nicole's mind. Not that she ever thought she'd personally have anything to worry about. Until now.

"Where were you at 3:00 this morning?"

She didn't think it was a good idea denying she'd left her cabin. For all she knew, the ship was equipped with security cameras.

"My plane arrived late last night. I couldn't sleep, so I took a walk around the deck. I thought the fresh air would do me good. I went down to the main deck for a walk." She did her best to look Kolkov in the eye, speak in a low voice, and appear calm. He was sure to recognize the body language of someone who was lying.

"And who else you see on this 'walk'?"

"No one."

"You hear anything?"

"I heard a scream when I was on my way up to my cabin. That's why I turned around and went back to the main deck."

He gave a grunt that could have meant anything. "What your occupation?"

"I'm a private detective."

"You help police solve crimes?"

She was pretty sure he knew what she did, but she explained anyway. "No. I'm not in law enforcement. I do work for law firms and corporations. Sometimes we track down money people have hidden to avoid paying court-ordered judgments. We find and interview witnesses for lawsuits. We're called in to investigate when a company is accused of misconduct."

"No crime work?"

"Rarely. We usually leave that to the police."

He narrowed his eyes. "I see." He stared at her for a good long while, saying nothing. Her face felt hot, and she wondered if she was blushing. Was he making up his mind about her or waiting for her to say something that might be incriminating? Finally, he stood, pulled out a business card, and jotted something on the back before handing it to her. "You remember more, you call."

"Of course." She stood and, heart thumping in her ears, walked him to the door.

As soon as he was gone, she went into the bathroom and sent another message describing his visit.

"I have a hunch he'll be back, and I'm feeling pretty vulnerable here. Please call me."

The interview with Kolkov had felt ominous, especially since she had to deny that she'd witnessed the murder. She wondered what the intelligence agency was prepared to do to protect her. This was a question she should have asked in the first place. She thought about Davies and his description of this assignment as so benign that she'd have plenty of time to enjoy the tour. As far as she was concerned, witnessing the murder had already ruined the trip. These were dangerous people she'd been assigned to spy on, and the police were more dangerous still. What had she gotten herself into?

Chapter Three

THE GROUP'S FIRST TOUR HAD BEEN SCHEDULED for that day, a bus ride through Moscow for a historic overview, but it had been cancelled so the police could finish interviewing everyone on board. After Kolkov left, Nicole took a stroll around the deck, checking on the people she was supposed to be observing. All were accounted for, which meant Kolkov had finished interviewing everyone on A deck, and they were free to go about their business. A steady flow of police and crime scene techs visited the spot where the victim had been pushed to his death.

Her persons of interest were either eating alone in the dining room or on deck, buried in reading material or snoozing on a deck chair. No one was socializing with each other or fellow passengers with one exception—Mary Haworth, the woman she'd seen on deck the night before wearing a pink robe and matching slippers. Mary was carrying on a one-sided conversation with a woman in the next chair, who'd closed her eyes and appeared to be asleep.

Nicole was feeling groggy after her sleepless night. All at once, she was pulled out of her lethargy with the realization that she hadn't picked up her phone messages since she'd last left her office. She'd been so distracted getting ready for her trip, traveling, and dealing with the fallout from Swan's murder that she'd forgotten all about them.

Normally she checked her messages three or four times a day, hoping against all reason that she'd finally hear from Reinhardt. She pulled her cell out of her purse and put in the code for retrieving messages. A recorded message came on, explaining that her attempt to get messages could not go through because it came from a foreign country active in hacking electronic devices. To retrieve her messages, it said, she first had to call customer service to prove her identity. It gave an 800 number for her call.

When she tried the number, it wouldn't connect. That's when she realized an 800 number was for domestic calls and wouldn't work from Russia. This made her cranky. What fool had arranged this? If she was out of the country—for example, in Russia—she'd need an international number to reach customer service.

She tried using the cell's browser to find an overseas number for her mobile provider. There were several possibilities. She tried them all but each time got a hiccup-y sound that she assumed was either a busy signal or an indication she'd gotten the numbers wrong.

She spent nearly an hour pursuing this, but no matter what number she tried, it refused to go through. At last she gave up. She realized it was probably an issue with the international country code she was using and would take more research to figure out. It was too much to deal with when she was so sleepy. She promised herself she'd get back to it after she took a nap and had a clear head.

On her way up to her room, she felt her watch vibrate. The sensation was so slight, she wondered if she'd imagined it. Still, she went inside and pushed the buttons to receive a call. The sound that came out was barely audible. She pressed the watch to her ear and said, "Could you please repeat that?"

"Ms. Graves?"

"Yes."

"We received your report." The sound was so tinny, it was

impossible to tell if the speaker was male or female. "We're most impressed with your attention to detail, which is invaluable to us. Carry on. Don't worry about the police. These officers can be full of bluster. Rest assured that, in this case, the detective in charge knows nothing. You're perfectly safe. I have to keep this short, so I'm ringing off."

The caller was gone before Nicole had a chance to voice her objections to the way the assignment was going. She wasn't easily frightened and had handled dangerous situations in the past, but this felt different. She was on foreign soil, knew no one, and didn't speak the language. She couldn't even trust the police. What had been bothering her most, she realized, was her lack of control over the situation. If she was suddenly in danger, where would she turn?

The call had been somewhat reassuring. It showed that at least someone was monitoring the messages sent from her phone and would return a call for help. Her real problem, she decided, was her unrelenting jetlag. She was too tired to think straight. The most sensible thing to do would be to take a nap.

The ship's loudspeaker woke her around 5:00 p.m. It was Kolkov's voice ordering all passengers to appear in the entertainment arena on the main deck in thirty minutes. The large room served as a bar, dance floor, casino, and venue for entertainers. Still groggy, Nicole dragged herself out of bed and dressed. She was in time to find a spot in the first row.

Kolkov stood at the front and waited until the place was full before he spoke. "Police leave ship now," he announced. "But we not finish investigation. Our engineers look at evidence and decide if this…" He paused to consult his notes. "…Derek Swan jump or someone push him. Ship must remain in Moscow until we decide." As he left, the audience was abuzz. They were supposed to cruise up the Volga to St. Petersburg, stopping at points of interest along the way. How long were they going to be delayed? Would the cruise line compensate them for the interruption in the promised itinerary? When they grew tired of speculating, most of them remained in the big salon, heading for the bar or the slot machines.

When Nicole returned to her room, she made herself a double espresso, hoping the caffeine would clear her head. She went out on her deck to drink it. She sat there only a brief time before a cold fog rising from the river drove her inside. She turned on the TV. *RT News* seemed to be replay the same news it ran earlier, but even this was better than leaving her mind free to revisit the murder. After watching *RT*'s anti-American propaganda for a while, she decided that going down to dinner might be a more pleasant diversion, even if she wasn't hungry. She changed into fresh clothes and headed downstairs.

Instead of sitting at a large group table and mingling, as passengers were encouraged to do, Nicole chose a table for two. This would allow her to privately observe the people whose faces and identities she'd memorized. She'd only been seated a few minutes when a woman stopped at her table.

"Do you mind if I sit with you?" she said. "Unless someone's joining you, of course."

Nicole was surprised by the request. The fact that she'd chosen a small table should have been a hint that she wanted to dine alone, but she didn't want to be rude.

"Of course not," she said. "Please, have a seat."

The woman had long, dark, wavy hair and was quite lovely. She was dressed in a black, peasant-style blouse pulled down around her shoulders and a print skirt that fit closely to the hips then flared out at the bottom.

"I'm Katarina Heikkinen. Please call me Kat. All my friends do." The woman gave a warm smile. Her accent was so slight, it was hard to tell what her native country might have been. "I don't want to sit at one of those big tables either. What a collection of bores!"

"I'm Nicole Graves." Nicole reached out to shake the woman's hand. "I'm just getting my first real look at them. My flight got in late last night, and I slept most of the afternoon."

"I didn't arrive until this morning," Kat said. "I guess you missed last night's excitement, too."

"Actually, I was here," Nicole said. "The head detective seems to think the victim might have been murdered. Now we're stuck in Moscow until the police figure it out. A plot worthy of Agatha Christie."

Kat's laugh was musical. As they talked, their conversation grew more relaxed. Kat had a rather exotic background. She was brought up in Finland until her early teens, when her parents divorced, and her mother, a New Yorker, moved back to Manhattan, where Kat still lived and worked. She was an investment advisor for one of the big banks. She seemed fascinated when Nicole said she was a private investigator and wanted to know all about it. After a waiter took their wine order, another appeared to explain the night's specials and find out what they wanted for dinner. Once that was taken care of, Kat resumed questioning Nicole about her work.

Their dishes were served. House salads for both, which included fresh corn and lobster. The main dish was beef stroganoff with potato dumplings. The food, which had sounded appealing on the menu, was disappointing—the salad drenched in dressing, the beef tough and dry. Nicole left most of it on her plate.

"Did you know that you and I are the only single women our age on the entire ship?" Kat said. "And not one eligible man." She shook her head regretfully. "I saw you coming out of the Regent suite earlier. I'm so jealous! That was my first choice, but it was already reserved—for you, I guess."

"Actually, I wasn't the one who booked it," Nicole said. "A friend of mine did then had to cancel at the last minute. Of course, there was no refund that close to departure, so she insisted on giving me the ticket. I was really surprised when it turned out to be so luxurious."

"Lucky you! Your friend must be rich."

"Let's put it this way," Nicole said, thinking of her sponsors. "Money isn't a consideration."

The waiters arrived to clear their plates and serve dessert, an unappealing slice of white cake. Nicole left it on the plate. She turned to Kat.

"What made you choose this tour? Are you a Russian history buff?"

"It was my ex's choice. No idea why he decided on it." She paused and made a sound, as if she were gulping back tears. "This was supposed to be our honeymoon."

"Oh, no! What happened?"

"He backed out two days before the wedding." Now she was crying in earnest. "He said he'd met someone else and was confused. He wanted more time to think it over. That was it for me; I wasn't going to wait around while he chose between me and some other woman. I'd used most of my savings for the wedding itself—of course I couldn't get a refund by then. He paid for this trip, and as you said, there are no refunds that close to the date. So he gave me the tickets and told me to invite a friend and use them myself. At first, I refused. But then I changed my mind. Why not enjoy all this luxury while I try to convince myself that I'm better off without him?" She blew her nose hard.

"Maybe he was doing you a favor," Nicole said. "But I'm sure it doesn't feel like it right now."

"Let's talk about something else, OK?" Kat said. "What do you think of our fellow passengers? I sat at one of the big tables at lunch. The conversation was mind-numbingly dull."

Kat pointed out several passengers who'd attracted her attention. There was a couple she called "the hat people" because they both were wearing odd hats. Nicole recognized them as two of her targets, Sheila Drysdale and Lucien Collins. Nowhere had her background information said they were a couple, but they certainly were posing as one. Sheila had on a black-and-white dress with a wide-brimmed, black-and-white hat that swooped up on one side. Lucien wore a gray tracksuit with an old-fashioned tennis hat. It had a tiny brim, and the crown was smashed in as if someone had sat on it. Every other man in the room had followed the ship's suggestion of "dressy casual," with slacks and a polo shirt, sports shirt, or sweater.

Kat seemed to enjoy inventing nicknames for people. She'd come up with some for other passengers. She called Tyler Brandt, the young man Nicole had spotted in the crowd the night before, "the bro." She nicknamed Mary Haworth, who had the look of a suburban housewife, "the hausfrau." David Wynn, one of the men who'd thrown Swan overboard, was "the grim reaper," a reference to his sickly appearance.

Next, Kat nodded toward a man at one of the bigger tables who was holding forth about his gun collection in a booming voice. She called him "the mayor." With a jolt, Nicole realized she recognized him, too. He was James Bartel, one of the men who'd killed Swan. Kat was eager to share gossip about him: "He's a former mayor of Lubbock, Texas, with the most grating accent you've ever heard. He loves making smutty remarks. What's really weird is his meek little wife laughs her head off as if she thinks he's a great wit. He's always joking that the woman he calls the '*femme ancienne*' is his girlfriend." She stopped to point out an elderly woman in a pale blue shirtdress that looked like it dated back to the 1950s. "He keeps inviting himself to her room for a little 'tit-a-tit,' as he puts it. You should hear the things he says. Oh, he's horrible." Kat dissolved in laughter. The man may have been horrible, but she certainly found him entertaining.

Kat went on about other passengers. Her comments were amusing and sometimes witty, if a bit mean spirited. Nicole was only half listening as she looked around. Six of her remaining seven targets were in the dining room tonight. Only one, a woman named Gina DeSoto, hadn't appeared, although Nicole had seen her on deck that morning.

All the A-deck passengers were together for the 7:00 p.m. dinner seating, and Nicole, presumed, would share the same tour bus. That explained why whoever scheduled her trip had placed her on A-deck, which had the priciest accommodations, although it was a mystery why they'd chosen the largest and most expensive suite for her.

"Is that a smart watch you're wearing?" Kat said. "It's very pretty."

Nicole glanced uneasily at the watch, which she'd thought was ordinary enough not to attract much notice. "It's smart enough to tell me what time it is. But no, it's just a plain watch. I picked it up at a consignment boutique in L.A. I think it's quite old."

"But look how thick it is," Kat insisted, "And it has a knob and a button on one side, just like an Apple watch."

"Well, if it has any smart features, it hasn't revealed them to me."

"Look on the web. Maybe you can download instructions."

"I don't think so. I don't see even see a brand name," Nicole said.

"It might be on the back. Do you mind if I take a look?"

Nicole did mind. She was trying to think of a way to distract Kat's attention from her watch when a disturbance started up in the center of the room. David Wynn, aka the grim reaper, had been making his way toward the exit, leaning heavily on his walker. As he passed by former mayor James Bartel's table, Bartel's wife gave out a loud yelp. Bartel jumped to his feet.

"You stomped my wife's foot with your stupid goddamn walker," he yelled. He took a swing at Wynn, landing a solid punch on the jaw. Wynn keeled over. People at other tables jumped up and came forward to help, but Wynn angrily shooed them away.

"Leave me alone! I can get up myself."

Wynn put his hands on the mayor's table to pull himself upright, took a step toward Bartel, and punched him in the face. As Bartel went down, his wife emitted another shriek of distress. Wynn leaned over to pick up his toppled walker and headed for the exit at a pace he didn't seem capable of moments before. He'd already reached the door before Bartel was on his feet. His nose was bleeding. A waiter helped him to his chair and handed him a pile of cloth napkins to staunch the flow. Moments later, the maître d' bustled over with a bag of ice and stood there, talking to Bartel in a low voice. Nicole had the feeling he was telling the mayor that a fist fight in the dining room was unacceptable behavior on the *Queen of the Volga*.

"Well, he stomped my wife's foot!" the mayor half shouted.

Nicole turned to look at Kat, who was watching the scene with great interest. "That certainly caps an eventful day," Nicole said. "I'm beat, so I think I'll head back to my cabin."

Kat was still staring at Bartel's table, as if hoping for more action. She nodded without looking at Nicole.

"I'll see you on the bus tomorrow," she said. "Save me a seat if you get there first."

"OK," Nicole said, although she wasn't sure this was a good idea. She'd found Kat a pleasant dinner companion, but maybe it was better not to pair up with a passenger quite so interested in other people's business. In a way, she and Kat were alike. Kat was curious about people just like Nicole. And she was an excitement junky, another characteristic they shared. The woman might have made a good traveling companion another time. On this trip, however, Nicole was supposed to focus on observing her fellow passengers, not pairing off with another traveler given to constant chatter. She decided to arrive at the tour bus early so she could sit with someone else.

She thought about the behavior of her targets at dinner. They certainly weren't trying to blend in as she'd expect if they were up to something serious enough to attract the interest of British intelligence. These people were acting as if they wanted to call attention to themselves. Did they imagine this would make them seem less suspicious? She let herself into her suite and used her watch to send another report, detailing Gina De Soto's absence and what had happened at dinner. This raised a question in Nicole's mind. Had Gina, like Derek Swan, met with foul play?

§

At 7:30 the next morning, Nicole—certain that arriving at the bus a half hour before the tour's departure would be early enough to beat Kat—found the woman already on board, saving a seat for her. There was no way around it. Kat would be her companion for the day.

Kat greeted her with a big smile. "I'm so happy we ran into each other last night. I was afraid I wouldn't have anyone to hang out with on this trip. But as soon as I saw you, I knew we were going to be friends."

Nicole said she was glad, too, keeping her reservations to herself. Kat's need to talk all the time was a distraction, but Nicole was pretty sure she'd be able to keep an eye on her subjects. As the bus filled up, she was relieved to see almost all of them were there. The only exception was Gina DeSoto, who was still missing.

As the bus driver closed the doors, a young member of the ship's crew told them he was to be their tour guide. His name was Boris, and his English was excellent. He talked a bit about how much he enjoyed his job.

"At first it was hard to get used to American tourists because you smile so much." He was smiling as he said this, as if their tendency to smile was contagious. "You may notice that most Russians won't smile back at you. This is part of our culture. We smile only at people we know well and only if there is something to be happy about. Russians tend to think that someone who smiles all the time is insincere, hiding their true feelings. Some even consider a smile from a stranger rude. You might keep this in mind when you go into shops and restaurants. Don't expect waiters and salespeople to smile at you, and try not to smile too much." He gave a laugh as if he knew this was probably impossible.

This made Nicole reflect on her own behavior, the way she'd been trained to smile since she was little, just like most other Americans. Eventually, smiles became automatic, a habit generated by grown-ups' prodding. "Why are you looking so sour?" they would say, or "Where's that pretty smile?" or "What happened to those adorable dimples?" Later, when she was in her teens and early twenties, the demand for a smile was a form of sexual harassment directed at young women. "Smile!" she'd hear from a perfect stranger on the street. She had a friend who'd retort, "Kneel!" But that wasn't Nicole's style. She'd pretend to ignore it, even though she found such comments annoying and downright insulting. Was it possible the Russians were on to something?

Boris went on to explain that the drive into central Moscow would take an hour and a half because of traffic. He also mentioned that construction was going on in Red Square in preparation for a military parade on May 9, known as Victory Day. This was Russia's annual celebration of the defeat of Nazi Germany in 1945.

Many of the buildings they passed on the way were in the Stalinist style, massive structures, some topped with spires. He pointed out those of interest, the headquarters of the Federal Security Service, which replaced the KGB; Moscow Police headquarters; and various government agencies. Most interesting to Nicole was the centralized press building, where international as well as domestic media outlets were all housed.

Once they entered Red Square, Boris stopped them so he could point out sites of interest. Most of the group pulled out their cell phones and cameras to take photos. The gate they'd entered was an extension of the many-spired state history museum. The square itself wasn't square at all but a long, irregular rectangle formed by the buildings surrounding it. To their left was a huge Victorian structure that housed the famous GUM department store. At the far end of the square was St. Basil's Cathedral. But what stood out was the bustling activity along the entire right side of the square, where workers were preparing for the May 9 parade. The half-built bleachers looked as if they could accommodate thousands. A short distance behind the construction was the high wall of the Kremlin. The work wasn't fenced off from the rest of the square, but guards were stationed every twenty feet or so in front of it.

Sitting incongruously in the center of all this was the squat, old-fashioned building that housed Lenin's tomb. Despite the ongoing construction surrounding the tomb, it was still open. A sizeable crowd snaked out in front, waiting to get in. When Nicole and her fellow passengers saw the long queue, they voted to skip the tomb. Boris led them to the far end of the square and the colorful onion domes of St. Basil's.

While they waited to enter the cathedral, Boris told them some of its history, which both fascinated and horrified Nicole. Ivan the Terrible, the czar who'd commissioned the building of St. Basil's in the sixteenth century, rewarded its architect by having his eyes put out. This was to assure he'd never design a building more beautiful. The cathedral's interior was as ornate as the outside. Its carved wooden walls were painted in the same vivid colors, although there was more use of gold leaf inside. Religious paintings lined the walls. As she took in the building and its beauty, she couldn't help but think of its architect's gruesome fate and how aptly Ivan the Terrible had been named.

Leaving the cathedral, Nicole spotted a folded-up walker leaning against a fence nearby. She recognized it as Wynn's—an upscale model with a basket underneath and a seat that could be folded down when the user wanted to sit. Thinking back, she realized she hadn't seen Wynn since they entered the cathedral. As they headed toward the square's other sites, she noticed that all the people she was supposed to be watching had gone missing. They must have slipped away when the tour group entered St. Basil's.

Nicole kept looking for the missing passengers, but they were nowhere in sight. She and the others who remained were led through the state museum and several other buildings, ending up at the GUM mall. Boris gave them forty-five minutes to explore the ornate structure's warren of shops. Some were uniquely Russian, but many bore the names of international designers and more casual brands that could be seen in any American mall.

Kat led Nicole into a candy shop that had caught her eye and picked out a box of chocolates. But when she approached the counter, the salesgirl—busy talking on her cell—waved her away.

"Excuse me!" Kat said. "I want to buy this."

"I am sorry, madam, but we close for mid-day meal."

At this point, Kat showed an aggressiveness Nicole hadn't seen before. She argued with the woman, angrily pointing out that the shop was obviously open and that salespeople were supposed to stop what they were doing to wait on customers. Fuming, she slammed the box on the counter and told the woman, "In our country, you'd be fired."

The woman said something into the phone. It was in Russian, but her snide tone and the way she glanced in their direction made it clear she was mocking Kat or perhaps both of them. As they left the shop, Kat said, "I'm going to search this mall until I find someone to report her to."

"Let it go," Nicole said, glancing at her watch. "Our shopping time is up. We'll have to hurry to meet the others or they'll leave without us."

Still venting, Kat allowed herself to be guided down the escalator and out of the mall where the others were gathered.

By now it was past 2:00 p.m. and the end of their visit to Red Square. Boris sent them off to find a place to eat a late lunch.

"Be back at the bus no later than 3:00. We must leave at that time so we reach the ship before rush hour. If you aren't back before we leave, you'll have to take a taxi." He paused to point out an elegant nineteenth century building a few blocks away. "One of the doormen at the hotel will find a taxi for you. Some drivers don't like to stop for tourists."

As they walked toward the gate, Kat looped her arm though Nicole's and steered her across the street. "I read about a trendy hamburger spot on the ride in and found it on my map. It's not far." It was a ten-minute walk to the restaurant, a large storefront with high tables and yellow bar stools. The casual eatery was roomy enough to also house a museum of old Soviet arcade games. The burgers were served on black buns, much like Russian black bread. They came with a generous box of fries that reminded Nicole of home.

"Wait," Kat said, pulling out what looked like black cloth sealed in plastic. It had been folded inside the napkin. "What on earth is this?"

Nicole pulled hers out, too. "Oh, I read something about it. Russians think it's unsanitary to eat with their hands, which it probably is. Then high-end burger spots like this came into vogue, and they started giving away plastic gloves with the burgers. We're supposed to eat wearing these gloves."

Both the women put on the gloves and picked up the burgers. Aside from the meat, the filling included fried cheese, bacon, and sauce. "Oh, my God," Kat said after her first bite. "This is the best burger I've ever had." Nicole got up to fetch more napkins. Even so, both women ended up with spots of sauce on their clothes.

By the time they were done, it was 2:45. They had fifteen minutes to get to the bus. As they exited the restaurant, Kat pulled out her phone and consulted the map. The directions said they were to turn left to get back to the bus parking lot and that it was a ten-minute walk.

"Are you sure?" Nicole said. "I think we came from the other direction."

Kat studied the map on her phone and looked both ways. "I can't remember. But the map is usually right. Is it OK with you if we do what it says?"

"Sure," Nicole said. "But I've found online maps are sometimes off, especially in foreign countries."

They walked for quite a while but saw no sign of St. Basil's domes or the Red Square parking lot. "You were right," Kat said. "The map sent us the wrong way. Let's go back to the hamburger place and go in the other direction."

They walked as quickly as they could, but as they approached the lot, they could see the bus had already left.

"I'm so sorry," Kat said. "You were right about the map. I should have listened."

"Don't worry about it," Nicole said. "We got to test the map's accuracy in Moscow, and it failed. Next time we'll know."

When they entered the lot, they found David Wynn sitting on his walker, smoking a cigarette. Apparently, he'd missed the bus, too. He didn't seem to recognize them, or if he did, he was pretending he didn't.

Nicole wondered what had happened to the others who had slipped away from the tour. "You're on the *Queen of the Volga*, right?" she said.

"Correct." He didn't bother to look at her. He was staring up the street as if expecting someone.

"We got left behind, too," Nicole said. "We're about to have a hotel doorman hail a cab to take us back to the ship. Would you like to join us?"

"I already sent for a car. You can come along if you want." His tone was neither friendly nor unfriendly but flat with indifference.

"That would be great," she said. "Thanks!"

After a nod in her direction, he continued smoking his cigarette and looking around.

Kat took a step toward him. "I noticed you left the tour back at the cathedral. Where did you go?"

Wynn gave her a surprised look. "Pardon me?"

"You left your walker outside the cathedral when the tour started, and I didn't see you after that. I just wondered what you found more interesting than St. Basil's."

He paused and seemed to be reaching for an answer. "I had the address of a Russian—uh—antique dealer. So a group of us went out there to do some shopping."

"How exciting!" Katrina said. "What did you buy? Can we see?"

He held up his hands to indicate they were empty. "I had my purchases sent on. I don't have room in my bags, and the authorities don't like to see some of these things leave the country."

They waited quite a while with no sign of the van that Wynn had summoned. He called in after the first half hour, then reported to the women that it was the beginning of rush hour and the vehicle was stuck in traffic. They waited an hour before a shiny black minibus pulled up. The driver got out and helped Wynn into the front seat, placing his walker in back. Nicole noticed the vehicle had eight seats. Had Wynn been expecting the others in the group to show up?

The two women climbed into the second row of seats. They chatted quietly while Wynn, his head resting against the passenger window, appeared to be asleep. During the long ride back to the ship, Nicole was somewhat in awe of Kat's chutzpah, asking Wynn what he'd been up to. Nicole had the same question, but under the circumstances, it wouldn't do for her to be openly curious about her targets' whereabouts. And she was pretty sure Wynn hadn't gone anywhere near a Russian antique dealer. Since he was already lying about his identity and being disabled, she was disinclined to believe anything he said.

CHAPTER FOUR

EVENING TRAFFIC WAS AT A CRAWL, and the minibus didn't get Nicole, Kat, and Wynn back to the ship until well after 9:00 p.m. Dinner was long over.

Nicole was hungry, which surprised her after her late, filling lunch. Back in her suite, she got out a menu and called room service. The call went directly to the main desk. "I am sorry, madam," the night manager said. "Food service has closed for the night."

Nicole was surprised. This was billed as a luxury cruise. Didn't luxury cruises come with twenty-four-hour room service? But maybe this was just another quirk of Russian hospitality. "Couldn't they just make me a sandwich? I'll go down to the kitchen and pick it up myself."

"I am sorry, madam. Kitchen is closed." There was a click, and he was gone.

Nicole searched the refrigerator, locating several packets of cheese and crackers and a Cadbury bar. It wasn't much of a meal, and she was still hungry. Despite her fatigue, she made another attempt to get her phone messages. This time, the international number worked, and she was put through to customer service, only to be put on hold. She held the phone to her ear while she got ready for bed, then took it into bed with her. She fell asleep with the phone next to her ear, still on hold.

Her sleep was fitful, haunted by the scene she'd witnessed that first night. In her dream, she was the one being thrown off the ship, her body bouncing with the impact of hitting the water. She felt the current drag her down and tried to fight her way up to the surface. At that moment, the dream, which had seemed so real, burst like a bubble. She was sitting up in bed, struggling to breathe. By the time she realized it had been a dream, she was wide awake, still trembling.

Her duvet was on the floor, along with her phone, which was—predictably—out of battery. She put it on its charger and retrieved her iPad from the nightstand, resigned to spending the rest of the night reading. At some point, she must have dropped off, for the ring of the cabin's phone startled her awake.

"Hello?" she croaked.

It was Kat. "You sound like you're still asleep. The bus is leaving in forty-five minutes. If you want breakfast, you'd better get down here."

Nicole was immediately out of bed. She quickly washed and got dressed, grabbing her coat and purse on her way out. When she arrived in the dining room, it was almost empty. The waiters were carrying away the last of the buffet's hot trays. Kat had saved her a pastry and a cup of coffee. It was clear that Nicole would have to spend another day in non-stop conversation with Kat. She wished the woman hadn't latched onto her. Kat seemed determined to be Nicole's best friend and constant companion. This was a problem Nicole hadn't encountered since middle school.

By the time Nicole and Kat arrived at the bus, it was almost full. All of Nicole's targets were on board, even Gina DeSoto, the woman who'd been missing from the tour the day before. In the photo Nicole had seen, Gina was an attractive brunette of a certain age with a kittenish smile. This morning, her expression was grim, and she gave off a negative vibe, as if to warn people away. She was wearing a great deal of makeup, which did not improve her appearance.

Today they had a different guide. This one was a local, who didn't work for the cruise line. When the travelers noticed the bus pulling into the parking for Red Square, they told him they'd already been there the day before.

"I show you different parts other guide not know," he said. He was young like Boris, their guide on the previous day, but this man didn't have Boris's friendly, outgoing personality. He didn't bother to introduce himself and was unyielding in his determination to give them a second tour of the square. As they entered, Nicole noticed more construction in progress. Some of the bleachers were almost complete. Workers were busy making chalk marks on the ancient stone pavement in front of Lenin's tomb. Heavy electrical cords snaked near the construction, making the area hard to navigate.

At the guide's insistence, they began at the tomb. "Is closing soon for builders finish platform for speakers," he said. "I make special arrangement for you to get in." Despite his "special arrangement," they had to wait nearly an hour to see the embalmed revolutionary. Nicole was amazed at how well-preserved Lenin's body was. He was also a great deal better looking than in the photos taken of him when he was alive. The guide mentioned that he'd been removed from the tomb for several years to undergo "restoration."

"I'll bet they made a wax-works copy and buried the real body," Kat whispered. "It would have been in bad shape after lying in state for nearly a century. Even ancient Egypt's embalmers weren't that good."

The guide started to steer them toward St. Basil's Cathedral, but the passengers objected so vociferously that he gave up. Taking advantage of their new-found power, they also insisted on a bathroom break. Once they congregated again, he led them back to the bus. Nicole was already seated when she noticed her targets weren't on the bus. She got up and went to the door to peer out. The group was nowhere in sight. She briefly considered getting off the bus to look for them, but what would be the point? She didn't know the area well enough to look for them without getting lost. And if she limited her search to Red Square, the bus would probably leave without her.

Only when she turned to go back to her seat did she realize Kat was standing behind her.

"What's wrong, Nicole?" she said.

"I left my lip gloss in the loo," Nicole said. "But it's not worth going back and risk missing the bus."

The tour guide waited another few minutes before muttering to himself and motioning the driver to close the door and move on. They drove through old Moscow, with its many onion-domed churches and spired, fortress-like structures. The guide didn't provide the usual tour-guide patter about what they were seeing. He seemed deeply offended by the group's rejection of his itinerary.

They hadn't gone far when she spotted the press building she'd noticed the day before. She wondered what was going on inside and what today's big story might be. Russian journalists would be in there along with foreign ones, including those representing major American news outlets. How could it not be an exciting place to work, located in the capital of one of the world's most watched and feared countries?

In the absence of input from their guide, Kat had taken out her guidebook and was reading aloud as they passed sites of interest. At last the bus parked, and the guide led them through the streets. He was in full pout, punishing the group with his silence. They walked through several museums where most of the signage was in Cyrillic, and they had only a vague idea what they were seeing.

Finally, they reached a museum of universal interest. It was dedicated entirely to vodka. The display included bottles representing hundreds—perhaps thousands—of brands of vodka, some in odd and fanciful collectors' bottles. A young woman with rosy cheeks and braids across the top of her head stood by the counter, holding a tray of paper cups. As the tourists filed by, she offered samples of two brands of vodka. One had an unpronounceable name and was flavored with ginger. The other brand was Putin Vodka, though Putin himself was reputed to be a teetotaler. Not surprisingly, Putin Vodka was produced by a state-owned distillery. Nicole took a few sips of each and put the cups down. The portions were more than she was used to, especially on an empty stomach. Lunch hour was long past. After her light breakfast, she was starving.

Just outside, a stand was selling assorted sausages and kabobs. They bought long sausages on buns, and Kat insisted on paying. Oddly, despite the fact that they were on buns, the sausages were mounted on skewers. Dressed with mayonnaise and jam, they were delicious. Some of the group was still in the shop, buying vodka to bring back to the ship. At last, they all boarded the bus again. It took them through Moscow's new financial center, where gleaming skyscrapers towered above the rest of the city. Soon they got off the bus to ride Moscow's Metro, stopping at Kiyevskaya, considered the system's most beautiful station. It was an art museum in itself, filled with large oil paintings inside ornate plaster frames built into the walls.

Around 3:30, they were ushered back on the bus to return to the ship. None of the missing passengers had made an appearance. This was understandable. Even if they'd wanted to, they wouldn't have found the bus, which was now far from Red Square.

They arrived back at their destination two hours later. Both Nicole and Kat retired to their cabins for a rest. Nicole, feeling drowsy again, was hoping for a quick nap before dinner. But first she had to send a message reporting that the group had left the tour again, and she'd been unable to follow them.

Before she had a chance to do that, someone knocked on the door. Nicole felt a shiver of alarm. Could it be Colonel Kolkov back for another interview? She held her breath as she went over to look through the peephole. To her surprise, it was Kat, even though they'd parted no more than ten minutes before.

Kat looked as if she'd been crying. "I hope I'm not being too much of a pest." Her voice was shaky. "But Jack just called. He's having second thoughts about his second thoughts. I hung up on him. I really need someone to talk to." Kat was crying in earnest now.

"I'm so sorry," Nicole said. "Come in. I'll make you a drink, and we can sit down and talk about it. Would you like a glass of wine?"

Kat snuffled into her tissue and reached in her purse to pull out another. "I think I need something stronger." Her voice was thick from crying. "Do you have ingredients for a martini?"

"Sure thing."

Kat moved past Nicole and was standing in the middle of the room. "I'm so sorry to barge in on you like this. I hope you don't mind." She turned around to take in the decor. "Your suite is beautiful. Do you mind if I look around?"

"Go ahead. Take a quick tour while I fix the drinks."

Nicole felt sorry for Kat. What a creep this fiancé must be. She didn't mind lending her new friend a shoulder to cry on, but she had to send that message to her handler, and she couldn't do it with someone else there. When she thought about it, the message didn't seem that urgent. After all, the group had done the same thing the previous afternoon. She'd reported it. As far as she could tell, nothing had been done. It could wait until after dinner.

While Nicole mixed the martinis, Kat wandered around. She was in the rear of the suite for so long that Nicole went to find her. Kat was washing her face in the bathroom.

"The drinks are ready," Nicole said.

"This suite is fabulous." Kat was patting her face dry with a clean towel. "What I have is basically a studio. It's big for a ship's cabin, but the bed is part of the living room, and I don't have a walk-in closet or a bathroom done in Carrara marble."

When they sat down with their drinks, Kat looked at Nicole and her eyes teared up again. "I just don't know what to do. Jack says he's just realized that he loves me after all and wants me back. He's such a jerk! I still love him, but how can I trust someone like that? If he left me once for another woman, he'll do it again. Don't you think?"

"I don't know Jack," Nicole said. "But commitment is really hard for some guys, and maybe he was just having a moment because he was scared. Obviously, this is your decision. If you think it's worth giving him another chance, you could take him back and see what happens. But you may find yourself suspicious of him all the time, imagining him cheating on you or looking for someone better to come along."

Kat shook her head. "I don't know. I guess I'll have to consider it." There was a long silence while she seemed to be doing just that. But apparently her thoughts had slipped back to her favorite topic, speculation about the odd behavior and shortcomings of their fellow passengers.

"I forgot to tell you," Kat said. "I had a long talk with Mary Haworth—you know, the hausfrau. Boy, does she love to gossip. She had some really juicy stories. One of the older men on the trip—I think his name is Clarence or something like that—yesterday, he walked into the main deck women's room just as Mary was getting ready to leave. This guy actually peed against the wall, as if he thought there was a urinal there. But what Mary was most outraged about was that he left without even washing his hands." Forgetting her tears, Kat giggled, all but restored to her old gossip-loving self.

When the time came, they left for dinner. Nicole was surprised to find her targets back from their unexplained excursion. They were standing by the door to the dining room, waiting for it to open. They looked rather pleased with themselves. Nicole was surprised when Kat turned to Mary Haworth and said, "I noticed you didn't join us after Red Square. Where did you go?" It was the same question she'd asked David Wynn the day before.

The woman gestured toward the hat people. "Lucien and Sheila came up with the best idea! They heard admission to the Bolshoi Ballet's practice sessions is free. There was one today, so a group of us went then stopped for drinks at this place called Dr. Zhivago. Such a beautiful restaurant! Wish we'd had time for a meal, but we had to get back to the ship."

As they listened, Nicole exchanged glances with Kat. They were both thinking the same thing. The story sounded made up—and since Mary was no actress—utterly unconvincing. Once again, Nicole had reason to wonder what they'd really been doing.

Dinner was much calmer than on the first night when Nicole and Kat had met. But halfway through the salad course, Nicole noticed her purse wasn't hanging on the back of her chair where she'd left it. In a bit of a panic, she got up and looked around the chair then under the table. It was gone.

"Maybe you left it in your cabin," Kat suggested.

"No, I'm sure I had it with me."

"You might be misremembering. I do that all the time. Check your cabin. Here," she said, starting to get up. "I'll go with you."

"That's not necessary. I can find it by myself." The words sounded harsh, even to Nicole, so she added, "But thanks for the offer."

She walked quickly back to her cabin. Fortunately, she'd dropped the key into her coat pocket when she left. She let herself in and looked around for her purse. It wasn't there. By now she was genuinely worried. Was there a thief on board? When she got back to the table, her purse was on her chair. She looked at Kat, who gave a big smile and gestured toward Tyler Brandt, sitting at the next table.

"The bro found it," Kat said in a low voice. "You know, he's not half bad. In fact, he's kind of growing on me."

Nicole was silent, quickly checking the contents of her purse. Everything was there—her phone, wallet, the little cash she was carrying.

By now, Tyler had noticed that Nicole was back. He got up and came over to their table.

"Thanks so much," Nicole said. "Where did you find it?"

"It was under the table."

"Funny. I looked there."

"I can see how you missed it," he said. "It got kicked to the side. But it's all good. Now I have an excuse to talk to the hottest chicks in the room. Maybe we can get together for a drink after dinner."

"Oh, yes." Kat gave him a dazzling smile. "Let's do."

"Count me out," Nicole said. "I'm really tired." She had no desire to have a drink with Tyler. For one thing, she was certain the purse hadn't been under the table because she'd taken a thorough look. Had he taken it so he could see what was in it? Why would he do that? In any case, if Kat was attracted to Tyler, she could meet him on her own.

Her thoughts were interrupted by a loud ding. She looked up to see the captain make the sound again, hitting his glass with a spoon to get the room's attention. He was late-middle aged, tall, and distinguished looking in his captain's uniform.

"I have bad news and good news." His accent was unmistakably Scottish. "Which would you like first?"

There were a few polite chuckles before someone called out, "Let's have the bad news."

"All right. Here it is. Because of the tragic accident on *Queen of the Volga* Tuesday night, the Moscow police have withheld permission for us to leave port. As you remember, our itinerary called for us to leave for our next destination in the morning."

Someone gave a loud boo. "But here's the good news," the captain went on. "We've arranged for you to have a free day to explore everything Moscow has to offer. Starting at 8:00, buses will be waiting to take you into the city center for a free day of exploration. We'll have shuttles back and forth to the ship every hour on the hour until 1500. Your tour guide, Boris, is at the door with a list of suggested walks and sites we didn't have time to cover in our city tours. We also have a pass that will get you into some museums and attractions free of charge. If you have any questions, I'll remain at my table after the meal."

As they walked out, they each took a handout and a museum pass. "I hear the evening entertainment is excellent," Kat said. "Please come with me. I'm not up for being alone right now."

"Weren't you going to have a drink with Tyler?" Nicole said.

"I don't think so. I don't know what happened, but he left the dining room before dinner was over. He seemed to be in a hurry. Please come! Staying up a little later might help with your jetlag."

"OK," Nicole said. "But first I have to go back to my room. I won't be long."

"You aren't feeling sick, are you?" Kat was all concern. "I knew we shouldn't have eaten that street food. Do you want me to come with you?"

"It's nothing," Nicole said. "I'm fine. I'll be right back. Save me a seat." She rushed back to her cabin, made her report, and returned to the event room. The evening's entertainment involved a troupe of acrobats, their act somewhat hampered by the small dimensions of the stage. When it was over, Nicole and Kat walked back to A-deck together.

Kat chattered about the performance and had more gossip about their fellow passengers. Nicole's mind was elsewhere. Wherever her targets were going tomorrow, she was determined to follow them. That would be impossible with Kat clinging to her. She had to figure out a way to escape from the bus before anyone else got off. In addition, the captain's mention of the police investigation had made her anxious. If Kolkov came back for another interview, she'd have to lie all over again. She just hoped she'd be able to keep her story straight.

Back in her suite, Nicole checked the time. It was 9:30 p.m. Once again, she was exhausted but not the least bit sleepy. She couldn't remember having a worse case of jet lag. This was her third night in Moscow, and her body clock was still completely off.

She turned on the TV and channel surfed, ending up on *RT*'s news feed. It was yet another rerun of the broadcast she'd watched earlier. She turned off the set and reached for her iPad to read *Little Dorrit*. She was approaching the end of book one, but she still had book two to look forward to. At this rate, she figured, the book was good for another two weeks of sleepless nights.

She'd just settled down to read when she noticed the low hum of conversation. It seemed to be coming from the deck behind her cabin. The moment she opened the sliding door to her private deck, a frigid wind blew in. She slid the door closed and put on her coat before stepping outside. By standing on one of the deck chairs, which was a bit wobbly, she was able to see the gathering. The seven people she'd been observing were all there, and an eighth person was just joining them. When the newcomer stepped forward to take a seat, Nicole was stunned to see it was Kat. What on earth was she doing there? The answer was obvious, but Nicole couldn't wrap her head around it. Kat—one of them? It seemed impossible, yet it made sense. This explained why Kat had been clinging to her, refusing to let Nicole out of her sight. Kat's story about the fickle fiancé had been a lie. Nicole felt stupid for being so easily taken in.

Nicole thought back to the moment someone brushed against her as she hurried away from the murder scene. It must have been one of the people gathered behind her cabin tonight. If it was, they'd know Nicole had witnessed the murder and must be afraid she'd tell the police. Clearly, she hadn't told Kolkov when he interviewed her, but perhaps they thought she still might say something—or be taken in by the police and forced to talk. They couldn't throw her overboard or silence her any other way. That would make the police double down on their investigation. Instead, they must have assigned Kat to keep an eye on her until they figured out what to do.

Her targets were talking in low voices. From her perch on the deck chair, Nicole could hear them. Kat herself was silent. David Wynn and Mayor Bartel seemed to be doing most of the talking. Nicole might have to be able to make out what they were saying if they'd been speaking English. But the language they were using was Russian, or perhaps Ukrainian.

Nicole hurried back inside to get her cell phone. She first set her watch to record. Then she turned off the flash on her cell phone and snapped a photo of the group. The overhead lights weren't very bright, and she wasn't sure it would come out, but it was worth a try. She turned on the recording feature. She'd send the recording on the watch to her handler, but the one on her cell was for her own use. She could put it through her phone's translation app in hopes that their conversation would give her some insight into what these people were up to. Her watch was on her left wrist, and she picked up the phone with her left hand. She climbed on the chair again and leaned against the outer wall of her cabin, where she'd be out of their line of sight. Steadying herself to keep her balance, she held out her left arm, directing the phone and watch so they were facing the group.

After about ten minutes, they got up to leave. They seemed on friendly terms. The women—including Kat—exchanged air kisses; the men hugged and backed pats. Even James Bartel, the mayor, and David Wynn, the grim reaper—the two who'd come to blows in the dining room—parted amiably. No doubt they'd faked the fight. They were pretending to be enemies, while the rest refrained from acknowledging each other in public. It was an act so no one would suspect they were in cahoots. Wynn was using his cadaverous appearance to feign weakness. She wondered if Bartel, the mayor, was faking the Texas twang.

Most of all, she was astonished that Kat could be allied with these people. Apparently, British intelligence had been unaware of her. Maybe she was a late addition, like Nicole herself. Kat might have been added after Derek Swan was killed.

She tried to translate the conversation she'd recorded on her phone. But her cell's connection was down, and she couldn't use the app without it. She put in a call to the night manager.

"I am sorry, madam. Police order Wi-Fi shut down."

"My cell phone can work without Wi-Fi."

"Yes. But police install—" There was a pause as he reached for the phrase. "—uh...block on phones."

"You mean a cell phone jammer?"

"Yes."

Nicole found this especially alarming. The police had, in effect, cut off the passengers' communications with the outside world. After hanging up, she wondered if this had to do with the murder or if the police suspected something else was going on. According to Davies, the communication device on her watch worked via satellite and didn't use a Wi-Fi connection. She had no idea if a cell phone jammer might affect it. She could only try. She sent another message explaining the Wi-Fi outage and cell phone jammer.

"I'm really concerned about what's going here. I have reason to believe the people I've been following are onto me. I need you to get me off this ship ASAP."

She lay awake until 2:00 a.m., when, at last, she felt the watch subtly vibrate against her wrist. She pushed the button, and the person with the tinny voice greeted her. He, or she, explained that they were sending someone to take her off the ship if she was determined to leave.

"An extraction like this takes time to arrange. The earliest we'll be able to do it will be tomorrow evening after dark. I doubt you're in any real danger in the interim. After killing Mr. Swan, these people would be too worried about the police to make an attempt on your life."

Nicole gave an aggravated sigh. "All right, if that's the best you can do."

"Meanwhile," the voice said, "I wonder if you'd be willing to continue watching your targets—discreetly, of course—and keep us informed. Yeah?"

She thought about it for a long moment. She'd be spending her day in public among other tourists. It seemed fairly safe. "I'll do it, but remember, I'm leaving this boat tomorrow evening, no later. Promise me."

"You have my word. I want to thank you, Ms. Graves. You have no idea what a great service you're doing us."

§

The next morning, Nicole forced herself to jog around the deck, hoping to clear her head. She was on her second lap, when someone behind her called, "Yoo-hoo! Wait for me!" Nicole turned to see Gina DeSoto, limping in her direction. She was wearing a beige, wide-brimmed hat cocked over one eye. It looked like something she might have borrowed from the hat woman.

Nicole stopped and waited. "We haven't actually met, but you're Nicole Graves, right?" When Nicole nodded, Gina went on. "I don't know if you heard, but the police took me in for questioning the morning after Derek's death. They asked questions about you." She paused to snuffle into a tissue.

"About me?" Nicole said. "What did they say?"

Gina ignored the question. "It was terrible. They grilled me for hours. They accused me of being a spy or a terrorist—maybe both. Then they tried to make me confess I had something to do with Derek's death. One of them pushed me so hard that I fell and hurt my knee. They also gave me this." She pulled up the brim of her hat to reveal a black eye, which was visible despite her thick makeup. "I was afraid they were going to kill me. I didn't confess, of course, because I didn't do anything. I loved Derek. We were talking about getting married." She dabbed at her eyes again.

"How awful." Nicole could see Gina had been through something traumatic, although she didn't completely buy this story. The information she'd been given didn't identify Gina and Swan as a couple. They were only posing as one. Finally, Nicole said, "Are you an American citizen?"

"Yes."

"Why don't you get in touch with the embassy? Tell them what happened. Maybe they can lodge a complaint so the police will leave you alone."

"Maybe." Gina sounded doubtful. "But the reason I stopped you was to warn you. I should have done it yesterday as soon as I got back to the ship, but I was feeling so terrible, and I didn't know which one you were. I just ran into your friend on my way to breakfast, and she pointed you out."

"Go on." Nicole was growing impatient with this drawn-out explanation.

"The police asked if I knew you," Gina said. "They wanted to know if I saw you engage in any suspicious activity. Things like that."

"That's crazy!" Nicole did her best to sound surprised, but she wasn't. Ever since she'd met Kolkov and he'd asked her about being a private investigator, she'd sensed he thought she was up to something.

"If I were you," Gina said, "I'd get off this ship as soon as

59

possible and catch a flight home. That's what I'm going to do—as soon as the police let the ship give our passports back."

"What do you mean? They can't withhold our passports. We have to bring them with us when we leave the ship for today's activities."

"That's true, but they're giving us some other kind of ID to carry until the police are done with us. They're making sure we don't leave the country. Be careful. I wouldn't want you to go through what I did."

They'd reached the entrance to the dining room, and Gina headed in for breakfast. Nicole decided to go up to her room and change out of her sweats while she thought things over. Was Gina lying about the police department's interest in her? She knew this group wasn't much committed to the truth. Once again, she thought of the person who'd brushed against her as she left the murder scene. It must have been one of the people she was watching. They knew she'd witnessed the murder and wanted her off the ship and out of the reach of the Moscow police. Were they trying to frighten her into going home?

Nicole went to the front desk to check out Gina's story about the passports. The purser was busy sorting name tags with little Russian flags on them.

"I'm going to use the shuttle to see Moscow today," she said. "Can I have my passport?"

"Sorry, madam. The police make us—" he paused to summon up the right word "—withhold passports. I give you special ID card so you can leave ship. If anyone stop you, you show card." He opened the safe where the passports were stowed and, after digging around, pulled out a stack of cards bound together with a rubber band. He handed one to her.

She looked at it. It was printed in Cyrillic and didn't seem to be personalized in any way. "What does it say?"

"Say police let you go ashore only if you stay with tour guide from *Queen of Volga*."

"But there is no guide. We have a free day."

The manager looked puzzled; she could tell he didn't understand. She tried again. "There is no tour today. Each person goes to a different museum or on a walk. We won't stay in one group." She showed him the list that Boris handed out the night before.

"No worry. Card Is good ID for Moscow."

As he closed the safe, she gave one last longing look at the stack of passports inside. "But this doesn't have my name on it. If the police stop me, how will they know who I am?"

He waved away her concern. "You rich tourist. Nobody stop you. Only problem if you try to buy ticket and leave Moscow."

"I see," she said. And she did. She had to trust that her handlers would have a quick means of providing her with a duplicate passport or come up with a plan to get her out of Russia that didn't involve a commercial airline.

CHAPTER FIVE

ONCE AGAIN, NICOLE ARRIVED at the bus to find most of the usual A-deck crowd already on board. The passengers seemed to be looking forward to exploring Moscow on their own, and a sense of excitement filled the air. Her targets were present. As usual, none—except for those who'd coupled off—were sitting together.

The seats were full except for the one Kat was saving for her. Of all the people Nicole least wanted to sit with, it was Kat. But Kat, unaware of Nicole's discovery, was in a chatty, upbeat mood—or at least pretending to be.

"Hey, you," she said as Nicole took her seat. "You're looking especially pretty today. What's in the bag?"

"An extra layer of clothes." Nicole did her best to sound as if everything was fine, but it wasn't easy. Kat's pretense of being friendly, even affectionate, was pretty transparent. Nicole wondered why she hadn't spotted it earlier. "It turned cold yesterday afternoon," she went on. "I want to be prepared."

"The notice on the bulletin board said it's going to be warmer today—fourteen degrees Celsius."

"That's—what?— the high fifties? Still pretty chilly for an Angeleno." Nicole gave a little shiver. In truth, her tote held a change of clothes that she planned to use to disguise herself. But first, she had to get away from Kat.

As the bus headed toward central Moscow, Boris walked down the aisle handing out more copies of the tourist destination list he'd distributed the night before. When he returned to the front of the bus, he picked up the microphone.

"We're stopping at the same lot near Red Square where we parked before. There will be bus service for passengers who want to return to the ship at 11:00 a.m. and every hour until 3:00." He spent the rest of the ride answering questions about the destinations noted on the sheet.

Instead of listening, Nicole was thinking about the quickest way to get off the bus and disappear. If she was to change in time to pick up the trail of her targets, she'd have to be quick about it.

They entered the huge parking lot filled with tour buses and waited their turn to pull into a parking space. Kat was still reading the tour sheet, her lips moving slightly.

"What do you want to see?" she said.

"I'm not sure." Nicole was poised to get up and dash to the front of the bus as soon as it parked.

Kat pointed to an item on the list. "This looks interesting, an underground bunker built to shelter Stalin in a nuclear attack. It says here it's packed with gas masks and cold war paraphernalia."

"Sure. Let's do that. Does it say how to get there?"

"It has the metro stop, but no directions from there."

"After we missed the bus that day, we know we can't trust the map on our cell phones." The bus had stopped, and Nicole was already on her feet. "Ask Boris for directions. Meanwhile, I need to dash to the loo." She pointed vaguely across the square. "I'll be right back."

Nicole apologized as she pushed her way by passengers who were trying to move into the aisle. When she got off, she could see Kat and her targets still on board, stuck in a major jam-up. Boris was stationed by the driver, where people stopped to ask him questions before they got off. Nicole had her next moves planned.

She hurried around the bus and entered the space between two parked tour buses that had already emptied out. Hidden between the two vehicles, she pulled jeans on over her slim black pants. She took off her jacket, replacing it with a gray hoody, which she zipped all the way up. She swept her hair into a ponytail, covered it with a baseball cap, and pulled the hoody up over that. To this she added oversized black sunglasses. She squeezed her purse and jacket into the tote bag.

All this took no more than a few minutes. When she reemerged, she took a broad detour around her bus. Most of the passengers were congregated nearby, still waiting for directions or consulting guidebooks. Kat was slowly turning around, looking mystified as she surveyed their surroundings. Nicole could tell she was searching for her. For an uncomfortable moment, Kat stared right at her but failed to recognize her.

With some dismay, Nicole saw that her targets had left the bus and were nowhere in sight. She ran to the lot's exit and spotted them a good distance ahead. They entered Red Square, walking fast as if they were late for an appointment. Each member of the group was moving independently, pretending they didn't know each other. David Wynn was no longer on his walker and easily kept up with the others. Nicole ran into the square, then slowed when she was a reasonable distance behind them.

The construction projects had progressed substantially since the day before, suggesting that work had continued through the night. The bleachers were all but completed. It was clear that a large grandstand would sit in front of Lenin's tomb, which was now closed to the public. Some kind of heavy blue drapery covered the sides of the grandstand and bleachers. Russian flags—each with the distinctive white, blue, and red horizontal stripes—flew overhead.

Maintaining their distance from each other, Nicole's group had reached the grandstand. Even though tourists were still allowed to move about freely inside the square, guards were stationed in front of the new structures to make sure no one got too close. These guards were armed with assault rifles.

Nicole took refuge nearby, behind the kiosk of a vendor selling souvenirs, mainly refrigerator magnets decorated with photos of Russian landmarks and small figurines of St. Basil's Cathedral and Lenin lying in state. From here, she had a good view of her targets. They were wandering around in front of the grandstand, pretending to snap photos with their phones. They looked like any other tourists overwhelmed by a huge and impressive landmark.

At that moment, someone called Nicole's name. She looked around. Kat was about twenty feet away, but she wasn't looking at Nicole. She seemed to be following someone else, a petite blonde wearing a jacket similar to the one Nicole had taken off and stuffed into her tote bag. Nicole stepped back into the shadows of the workers' portable toilets. There, she waited until Kat passed—still on the trail of Nicole's doppelganger. Only then did Nicole resume her position behind the kiosk.

In the brief time she'd been gone—no more than a minute or so—her targets were no longer in sight. Holding her phone up, as if she was looking to find the right spot for a selfie, she walked in one direction, then the other. Finally, she spotted Tyler Brandt. He was just turning into a walkway between the last bleacher and an ornate brick building facing the square. A guard standing nearby either didn't see him pass or deliberately ignored him.

Nicole hurried toward the spot where he'd turned and tried to follow him. As she drew near, the guard stepped forward and blocked her path. He shouted something in Russian that clearly meant "Get out!"

She backed off to put some distance between herself and the guard, then ducked behind another kiosk to keep watch. Before long, four workmen came out of the brick building's lower floor. They were pushing a large pallet of what appeared to be building materials covered with a canvas tarp. The guard stepped aside to let them pass. Like the other workers in the square, the men were dressed in tan jumpsuits with orange safety vests and red helmets. It took Nicole only a moment to recognize them as the male contingent of the group she was following—Lucien Collins, James Bartel, Tyler Brandt, and David Wynn.

She followed them back to the grandstand where they parked the pallet and pulled the tarp aside. It was filled with what looked like cinder blocks. Brandt leaned forward and picked up two armloads. Wynn punched him in the shoulder and said something. The young man quickly put them back on the pallet. Then, after looking around, he lifted two of the blocks feigning great effort, as if they were extremely heavy. The other men each took two. They all headed for the side of the grandstand, where draped blue canvas covered the entrance to the space beneath.

Approaching the nearest guard, Wynn carefully put his blocks on the ground, took a paper from his pocket, and held it out. The guard read it with close attention before handing it back. He gave a little salute and lifted the canvas to admit them to the space beneath the grandstand. The men passed inside and went back for more blocks. Once they'd hauled all of them under the stand, they remained there for a good three-quarters of an hour before reemerging to roll the empty pallet back the way they'd come.

As Nicole followed them, she wondered what the blocks they'd left off were made of. Cinderblocks were quite heavy. But the light weight of these—demonstrated by the way Tyler Brandt first lifted them—suggested they were made from a different material than the real thing. Someone could have used a 3D printer to create the blocks out of drugs or some kind of explosive material. Then it came to her. Her fellow passengers might be planning to sabotage the parade—maybe even blow it up. If she was right, hundreds, perhaps thousands, of people would lose their lives. She couldn't let that happen.

In terms of Russia's power structure, the stakes were extremely high. *RT News* had said that the Kremlin's highest dignitaries, including Putin himself, were going to attend. He'd be sitting at this very grandstand.

How had Wynn obtained a pass to bring building materials into the structure? Judging by the guard's response—the little salute—the document must have appeared official, handed down from someone high in government.

The four men she'd been watching rolled the empty pallet back into the building from which they'd emerged. Once again, the guard ignored them.

She waited a good while before the men came out of the building again. The guard glanced at them briefly, then looked the other way. Her targets had changed into their street clothes and were now heading back the way they'd come. They weren't making as much effort to keep their distance, although they still weren't talking or interacting in any way. She waited until they passed before she started following them. They were headed across the square to the GUM mall.

Once they reached the mall, the three women of the group—Sheila Drysdale, Mary Haworth, and Gina DeSoto—joined them with hugs and pats on the back. Greetings over, they went into the mall and filed into what looked like an expensive restaurant. A sign in front, written in both Russian and English, advertised caviar and vodka. Nicole watched through the window as the maître d' seated them in a large rear booth. Nicole settled at a table outside the entrance where she could watch through the window.

A waiter dressed in a suit and tie came out of the restaurant to hand her a menu. Below the Cyrillic description of each dish were English, French, and German translations. When she asked for a pot of tea, he cleared his throat and pointed to a note at the bottom of the menu. It stated that any order required a minimum of 1500 rubles. She got out her cell and typed the amount into her currency converter. 1500 rubles was twenty-one dollars—not too outrageous. She scanned the menu before ordering blinis with caviar and sour cream. She wasn't hungry, but what did it matter? She just wanted a place to sit until the group left. While the waiter went to get her food, she dictated an urgent message through her watch, describing what she'd just witnessed and the perpetrators' current location. For the first time, there was no double flash to confirm her message had gone through. She sent it again with the same result. Was it possible she was sitting in an area where it couldn't connect with the satellite? All she could do was wait and try again later.

Meanwhile, she had to wait here and see where her charges went next. She took off her baseball cap, tucking it into her bag and pulling out a brightly colored scarf, which she draped over her hair and secured in back, hijab style. She hoped this would change her appearance enough to allow her to continue being invisible, just another tourist among thousands. So far, she was sure they hadn't noticed her.

The waiter brought her order. She nibbled at the blinis. They were quite good, and she regretted eating such a big breakfast on the ship. She'd helped herself to pancakes with all the trimmings and was still full. She kept her eye on the group while she sat for an hour, then most of another. They were ordering more drinks when it occurred to her that they might not be going anywhere soon. They were in there celebrating whatever they'd accomplished that morning.

Just then, the waiter approached her with the bill. "I'm sorry, madam. You must place another order if you want to stay. Customers will be here soon for the mid-day meal."

With a sigh, Nicole picked up the menu again. She still wasn't hungry, and the choices were fairly limited—different varieties of caviar with the blinis. That was it. She ordered the same thing again and asked for a fresh pot of tea. The waiter raised his eyebrows at her barely touched plate before picking it up and hurrying off.

Looking in the window, she noticed with a start that the group had left the booth and was moving toward the door. She retrieved her purse from the tote bag. Fishing out her wallet, she located four 1,000-ruble notes. This added up to what she owed for the two orders plus an overly generous—and undeserved—tip, but she didn't have time to flag down the waiter and wait for change. She placed the money on the table and used her water glass to anchor the bills against the breeze.

After her targets came out, she waited perhaps twenty seconds before she got up to follow them. She'd barely passed the front of the restaurant when her waiter came barreling after her. "Madam, madam," he shouted. "You forgot to settle your bill, and you must pay for the second order, even if you leave before it's ready."

She pointed to the bills on the table. He scooped them up and went back inside. Her targets were headed for a shop down the road, which turned out to be a liquor store. She waited a few doors down until they came out carrying several full shopping bags. They walked quickly, cutting across the square. Nicole had to run to keep them in sight until she realized they were returning to the parking lot where they'd all started out that morning. She checked her watch. It was now 11:40. The bus was supposed to leave on the hour, which would be 12:00. This gave her just enough time to readjust her appearance so she'd look like she did when they'd first arrived. She quickly changed, then went back to wait with the others. When the bus departed, the only passengers were Nicole and her targets. Except for those who were pretending to be couples, they were sitting apart, pretending not to know each other.

By the time they arrived at the ship, lunch hour had passed. Nicole stopped by the snack bar to pick up a sandwich. Egg salad was the only choice left, which made her regret the blinis she'd left on her plate at the restaurant. She unlocked the door to her suite and headed for the table to put down her purse. At that moment, someone grabbed her from behind and clamped a hand over her mouth. She jammed her elbow into his middle, and he let out an *oof* sound.

"Don't scream," he whispered in her ear. "I'm your handler. My name is Chet Antonovich. Sorry about this. I had to be sure you didn't alert other passengers that you have an unannounced guest. Nod if you understand, and I'll let go."

She nodded. He released her and stepped away. She turned around to get a look at him. He was tall, six feet three or six four with sandy hair, a full beard, and wide-spaced blue eyes. He appeared to be extremely fit. He was dressed in a black zip-front jumpsuit with the ship's logo on the pocket, an outfit he'd no doubt nicked from wherever they stored uniforms for the maintenance crew. Because of his height, his pantlegs were several inches short.

"Your watch is malfunctioning." His accent was decidedly British. "We received a few words of a message you sent at 10:53 today, but we couldn't hear the rest, nor were we able to reach you to ask you to message us again. We gathered it was important. I'm here to find out what it was."

Nicole gestured toward the couch. "Let's sit down." Once they were seated, she told him all that had happened since she began following her targets that morning: the pallet of phony cinder blocks and the time the men had spent loading them under the grandstand, remaining there for the better part of an hour. She also described the group's jubilant celebration when they left Red Square.

"I think they planted explosives under the grandstand," Nicole said. "Ian Davies, the man who sent me here, told me not to involve the police even if my target group did something illegal.

But it seems to me we have no choice. We have to report this to the Russian authorities. We can't just stand by while hundreds or thousands of people die in an explosion we could have prevented."

"We can't let the Russians know," Chet said. "Our operatives will make sure the explosives are neutralized and, hopefully, removed from the site. There's time. The military parade isn't until Monday. That's four days from now."

Nicole frowned and shook her head. "I don't get it. Why is this the business of the U.K.? If you simply told the Russians, they'd take care of it."

"That's the last thing we'd want to do. It would set up a chain reaction that would kill a lot more people than can fill Red Square. I can see you need to have a better understanding of the situation. What I'm going to tell you is top secret. You'll be bound by our Official Secrets Act. You cannot tell anyone—not a living soul. Do you understand?"

"Of course."

"All right then. The eight people you've been observing are activists in FALGA, an extremist offshoot of the Ukrainian nationalist movement."

"Are these people Ukrainians?" she said. "How can that be? They all speak perfect English and are passing themselves off as American tourists."

"They've been preparing for this for years. That includes extensive training in English to perfect an American accent."

"They sure fooled me," Nicole said. "But please go on."

"The Ukrainian government's goal is to appease Russia," he said. "Above all, they want to avoid any action that would anger Russia and escalate the conflict between the two countries. FALGA, on the other hand, advocates violence. They're determined to get revenge for Russia's attacks on eastern Ukraine, which killed 13,000 Ukrainians since Russia invaded Crimea.

"If the Russian Federation were to learn that explosives were planted by Ukrainians in a venue where Putin is to appear, they would immediately retaliate. Russia would not distinguish between those who represent the Ukrainian government and an organization like FALGA, which works underground and has different objectives. They would bomb Ukrainian population centers or invade the country. In other words, we're talking about a possible war, and other countries would have to get involved. So it's in the interest of all of Europe to make sure this doesn't happen. For your information, the U.K. isn't the only country working on the operation. You can be sure we have experts capable of rendering these explosives harmless and untraceable to the Ukraine."

Nicole nodded her head. She was dumbstruck by the enormity of the operation in which she was playing a small role.

For the first time, Chet seemed to relax. "I have to ask one more favor. I need you to come to Red Square with me this evening so you can show me exactly where they left the explosives. Will you do that?"

"Wait!" Nicole said. "You promised to get me off the ship and out of Russia tonight."

"Yes, and we're set to do that," he said. "But first, will you show me the location of the explosives? It will delay your departure for a few hours, but you'll be doing us a great service."

"All right."

"Brilliant. I'll come by for you tonight around 11:00. Wear jeans or trousers of some kind."

"Won't the place be locked up and guarded at that hour?"

"It will be guarded, but they're behind schedule, so work continues twenty-four hours a day. I'll bring you a uniform and the credentials you'll need. Once you show me the location, my agency will take it from there. Again, you can't tell anyone what I just told you or about your mission here."

"I understand. You can count on me."

"I know I can. Now for your future plans, as of tomorrow, you will no longer be working on this assignment. You're free to continue the tour, but given the circumstances, I imagine you'd prefer to return to the U.S."

"You're right. I've had quite enough of Russia," she said. "I want to go home, but they're holding my passport."

"Don't worry about the passport. There are ways to work around it. You'll have to leave your things behind, I'm afraid. We won't be coming back to the ship. But you can send us an itemized list of clothing and other items, and the agency will reimburse you." He stood up. "Oh, I almost forgot." He pulled something out of one of the pockets in his jumpsuit. "I have a replacement for the broken watch." He held out what looked like a man's watch, a digital model, silver, on a leather band.

"Oh," she said. "It's completely different from the one I have. One of the passengers did notice it—" Nicole stopped, reminded of Kat and her sudden appearance with the FALGA group. "Her name is Katarina Heikkinen. Do you know her?" He shook his head, and she went on. "She appointed herself my traveling companion. Then last night I saw her meeting with the people I've been following."

"I've never heard of her," Chet said. "She is probably going by an alias. About the watch, sorry we don't have the same model. Since communication is vital to your mission and safety, we'll have to take a chance that no one will notice. Best wear a long-sleeved jumper or blouse and keep the watch covered."

Somewhat reluctantly, Nicole took off the rose-gold watch, handed it to him, and replaced it with the new one. She walked him to the door.

"Thank you for everything you've done," he said. "I'll see you tonight, yeah?"

After he was gone, she studied her new watch. She didn't like it much; it certainly wasn't pretty like the original. Then she noticed the time. It was 3:00 p.m. Kat might be back from the day's tour any time now. She'd probably seek her out, aggrieved at being deserted that morning. Nicole shrunk at the idea of having to continue playing dumb and feigning friendship as if she didn't know the woman had been spying on her. She'd already planned to plead illness as her excuse for abandoning Kat that morning. Kat had mentioned the possibility of food poisoning from the sausages they'd bought from a street vendor. This gave Nicole the perfect excuse. Only now did she realize that she'd forgotten a crucial step in making her excuse airtight.

She got her phone out of her purse and typed in a message to Kat, well aware that it wouldn't go out with a cell phone blocker in place. It explained that she was returning to the ship because she was ill. Then she left it in her out-box as if she'd forgotten to send it. This done, she decided to change so she'd look as if she'd spent the day in bed. She took off her boots, then went into the walk-in closet to get her pj's. The first thing she noticed was that the bottom drawer of the bureau was slightly open. When she'd unpacked, she easily fit all of her things in the top three drawers. She'd never opened the bottom one. She bent down and pulled out the drawer so she could see what was in there. Sitting in the otherwise empty drawer was a small, silver gun.

She stepped back and stared at it. Someone had been in her room and left this. Chet had been there, of course, but he would have told her if he was leaving a weapon. It had to be Kat, who'd spent some time exploring this part of the suite.

Nicole picked up the gun and took a close look. She recognized the model, which was designed to fit into a woman's purse. Even though Nicole hated guns, she owned one. After several close brushes with violence, she'd applied for a license to carry a concealed weapon. Her main criteria for choosing a gun had been its size. Was it small enough to fit in her purse and light enough to make it easy to carry? Once she had her license and the weapon, she made it her business to learn how to use it. She went to target practice regularly and had become something of a sure-shot.

Of course, she couldn't bring the weapon with her. Not only did TSA forbid guns on planes, Russia had very strict laws governing such weapons. Nicole had looked it up. Foreigners were forbidden to be in possession of firearms on Russian soil. That would have given someone—most likely Kat—a motive to leave the gun here. It would be easy for the police to find if they came back and searched the suite again. They'd haul Nicole off to jail and would no doubt refuse to believe that she had no idea who'd put it there.

She debated what to do. She knew there was nowhere to safely hide a gun in a hotel room, much less in a ship's cabin, even a spacious one like this. Maids came daily to clean and change the linen; management had access to the safe, and so did the police. Now, with the investigation still active, this gun was a huge liability.

The simplest way of dealing with it was to get rid of it. All she had to do was drop it in the river. She picked up the gun, went onto her balcony, and immediately realized her mistake. There were four ships lined up between *Queen of the Volga* and the dock. On the ship nearest hers, not fifteen feet away, two people sitting on their private deck were staring at her. She'd have to wait until dark so no one would see her toss the weapon into the water. She went inside and closed the door.

Back in the closet, she returned the gun to the drawer for the time being and got into her pj's, pushing the new watch as far up her arm as it would go. The sleeve easily covered it. She'd just put on the robe and slippers when she heard loud knocking at her door. Nicole's first thought was that Colonel Kolkov was back to question her again.

She dashed into the closet, took the gun out of the drawer, and looked around for a better place to hide it. The knocking got even louder, and she realized she couldn't waste any more time. She dropped the weapon into one of the boots she'd just taken off. She put the boots on the closet's shoe rack and hurried to the door.

Nicole peered out the peephole. It was Kat. Nicole took in a deep breath, part relief that it wasn't Kolkov, part apprehension at having to deal with Kat and pretend she wasn't on to her.

"What happened to you?" Kat was angry. "I looked all over. You disappeared, and it spoiled my whole day."

"I'm sorry." Nicole did her best to sound both weak and contrite. "I went back to the ship because I was feeling sick. I sent you a message. Didn't you get it?"

Kat pulled her cell out of her bag and checked it. "No!" She gave Nicole an accusing look and held out her phone. "See? No message."

"But I'm sure I sent one. Come in. I'm feeling—I need to sit down." She backed into the sitting room and dropped onto the couch. Kat followed but remained standing.

"I went to the loo when I got off the bus. Remember?" Nicole went on. "I was feeling sick. By the time I got out, I felt even worse. I didn't want to wait for the bus back to the ship, so I caught a cab. That's when I sent you the message." She reached into her bag, which was on the couch next to her, and took out her phone to locate the message.

"See? Here it is. Oh, no! It looks like it didn't go out. Maybe I forgot to hit the send button. I'm so sorry." She held out the phone to Kat, who took it and read the message.

"Oh, you did try to reach me." Kat's anger disappeared, and she was instantly all concern. "Is it your stomach?" And to Nicole's nod, Kat added, "You could have food poisoning. These Russian kitchens are filthy, and we ate those sausages from a street vendor yesterday. You'd better see the ship's doctor."

"I'm not sure what it is," Nicole said. "I'll see the doctor if I'm not better by tomorrow. Right now you'll have to excuse me. I need to lie down."

"Wait," Kat reached her hand out and touched Nicole's forehead. "I think you have a fever. This could be something serious, like E. coli. Stay here. I'm going to get the doctor."

Nicole's patience had reached the breaking point. "Don't you dare! I'm going to take a rest—an uninterrupted one. You have to—"

Her words were drowned out by someone pounding on the door. "Open up! Police!" She recognized Kolkov's voice and immediately thought of the gun in her boot.

She opened the door. Kolkov was there, flanked by two uniformed officers. He gave Nicole a cursory glance before his eyes fell on Kat. "The man at desk say I find you with this woman." Pointing to Kat, he turned to the policemen behind him and said something in Russian. Each grabbed one of Kat's arms. She struggled to pull away.

"What are you doing?" she shouted. "I'm an American citizen. Let go of me!" As they marched her down the corridor, she kept shouting. Several stateroom doors opened as they passed.

Kolkov watched them go, then turned back to Nicole. "Not worry. They just take her for formal interview." He stepped forward, taking Nicole's arm and leading her to the couch. "Sit," he said. "I look around."

Once more, Nicole thought of the gun stupidly hidden in her boot. Now she really did feel sick.

CHAPTER SIX

NICOLE SAT AND WATCHED KOLKOV look around her sitting room. After pausing to go through the drawers of the end table, he closely examined the lamp on top, turning it upside down as if he expected to find something hidden inside. When this didn't pan out, he moved onto the credenza and the cabinets above, working his way over to the small refrigerator under the wet bar. Only then did he notice the liquor sitting on the counter. He picked up a vodka bottle labeled "Beluga" and emitted a loud "aha" of pleased discovery. He got down a tumbler and poured himself a good amount, downing it in a single gulp. After he swallowed, he let out a long, exaggerated "ah" before setting the glass on the counter.

As he walked into her bedroom, and Nicole's stomach lurched. The minutes dragged by, and she found it impossible to sit still. All she could think about was the gun and how stupid she'd been to hide it in one of her boots. If Kolkov picked them up, he'd notice one was much heavier than the other. She expected him back any moment, holding up the gun and placing her under arrest. At last he emerged. To her great relief, he wasn't carrying the gun. Instead, he had her iPad, which she'd locked in the safe that morning. She wasn't surprised he'd have access to the stateroom safes. Of course the ship's management would have given the police the universal code to open them.

Sensing he expected a protest, Nicole said, "Why are you taking that? There's nothing on it but books and movies."

He gave her a look of defiant amusement—perhaps thinking of the power he held over her—before reaching for her purse, which was next to her on the couch. He took out her phone and put it on top of the tablet before handing the purse back to her.

"I go now. We see what is here." He held up the iPad and the phone. "Later I return."

After he was gone, she locked the door and retrieved the gun from its hiding place. She took it into the bathroom and opened the lid of the toilet tank. After wedging the gun behind the flushing mechanism, she replaced the lid. It was probably one of the places Kolkov would look if he returned and decided to give the suite a more thorough search. Hopefully, he'd stay away until after dark when she'd have a chance to toss the weapon in the river. She flushed the toilet to be sure it worked. Still trembling from the stress of having Kolkov search her cabin again, she paced a bit then decided to go out on her balcony. Maybe some fresh air would help her calm down.

The deck was sunny but chilly from the wind blowing across the water. She stood at the railing a while, studying the ship anchored next to hers. The few passengers outside were on deck chairs, covered with blankets. They appeared to be dozing.

Her mind turned to Kolkov and the devices he'd taken away—both her iPhone and iPad. He wouldn't find anything compromising on them. All at once, she realized she still hadn't been able to listen to her voice messages, and now that was out of the question. She remembered, suddenly, the blinking light on her office phone. She hadn't picked up messages from the office either. Even if she could find a cell to borrow, it wouldn't help—not if the ship had a cell phone jammer.

When dinner finally rolled around, she decided she might as well go down to eat. It would be a distraction from the long evening ahead, waiting for Chet to arrive. Besides, she was curious to see what her fellow passengers were really like. She couldn't believe they were as bad as Kat had made them out.

When Nicole entered the dining room, all of the seats were taken except for two singles at a large table where three of her targets were sitting—David Wynn; James Bartel, the mayor; and Mary Haworth, the hausfrau. Nicole had no choice but to join the group. Wynn was his usual enigmatic self, ignoring the people around him. He'd just finished refilling his wine glass to the very top. Red wine spilled on the tablecloth as he lifted it to his mouth. Mary and the mayor were deep in conversation, and Nicole detected a certain degree of tension between them. From the way they were slurring their words, it was evident they'd continued their celebration throughout the afternoon.

Nicole had no desire to enter the conversation. She focused on listening to the others and eating her salad, once again swimming in dressing. Her silence soon became a subject of comment for Mary and the mayor, moving from unfunny teasing and to an argument between the two. They didn't speak directly to her but referred to her in the third person as if she wasn't sitting right there.

"She's certainly a pretty little thing," the mayor said. "I'll bet she's broken a heart or two."

"Don't you notice how quiet she is?" Mary snapped. "Maybe her heart is broken. Did you ever think of that? Women have feelings, not that you'd ever notice."

"Well, there's a limp dick in this somewhere." His comment sent his wife into a fit of giggles, and he let out a snort of laughter at his own wit. Emboldened, he turned to address Nicole directly. "What is it, sweetie? You disappointed in love? Why don't you come sit on my lap? Once you get on, you won't ever want to get off."

Nicole put down her fork. "That's quite enough," she said.

"Oh, come on, love cakes. Can't you take a joke?"

"To qualify as a joke, it would have to be funny." Nicole got up and headed for the door.

"See?" Mary turned to the mayor accusingly. "You drive people away with your filthy mouth." As Nicole left the dining room, Mary continued berating him. The last thing Nicole heard was the mayor's booming voice, "What's with you, Mary? You going through the change? Let's ask the waiter to bring you some ice. You can drop it in your pants to cool off."

Nicole wondered if this was part of an act or if they were both simply mean drunks. She smiled with the knowledge that she would be gone well before dinnertime rolled around again. Kat had been right after all. They were dreadful dinner companions.

Back in the suite, the evening that stretched ahead seemed endless. Her first priority was to get rid of the gun. It was now 8:00 and quite dark. She removed the weapon from the toilet tank, took it out to her deck, and dropped it over the rail. As it disappeared into the dark water, she had an enormous feeling of relief. The cold quickly drove her back inside. She washed her hair and changed into as many layers of clothing as she could. It was going to be freezing out, and this would help her keep warm. She pulled on a black sweater over two cotton turtleneck T-shirts. Two pairs of leggings fit easily under her jeans.

By the time she was done, it was 9:00 with two hours still to go. There was nothing left to do but sit on the couch and read her book. Then she remembered that *Little Dorrit* was an e-book on her iPad, which Kolkov had taken. She felt a stab of loss. How could she get through the next three hours with nothing to read?

She left her suite and went down to the ship's library to look through a meager collection of worn paperbacks, probably left behind by other passengers. She found a lot of romances and westerns. Among them was a copy of Charles Portis's *True Grit*, which she'd enjoyed years before. She took it back to her cabin.

She was completely absorbed in the book when she heard three slow knocks at the door. She glanced at her watch, surprised to see it was already midnight. She got up and opened the door. Chet stepped inside and quietly closed it. This time he was dressed in the white uniform of the ship's service staff. It was a size or two too small. Not only were the sleeves and pant legs short, but the shirt was so tight that the fabric gaped between the buttons.

"Are you ready to leave?" he said.

"Ready." She smiled, happy the long wait was over.

"Brilliant. You'll need to put these on over your clothes." He handed her a plastic bag. Inside were a tan jumpsuit and orange vest, just like the workers' uniforms her targets had worn that morning in Red Square. Nicole put them on over her many other layers of clothing.

"Huh!" Chet said, after stepping back to take in her appearance. She could see he wasn't pleased. "I knew you'd need a small size. I guess I didn't realize you were this—" he paused "—um, small." Indeed, the pants covered her boots and extra fabric bunched halfway up her legs. The sleeves overhung her hands by a several inches. While she rolled them up, Chet dropped to his knees and rolled the pant legs. When they were done, she put on the vest.

He looked her over again and shook his head. "Not ideal, but I think we can make it work. You'd best hang back in the shadows once we get to Red Square. Get your coat. It's freezing outside."

She put her coat on over the jumpsuit and many layers of clothing, then followed him out of the suite. He led her to the other side of the ship and opened an unmarked door leading into a stairwell. Instead of the thickly carpeted stairs provided for passengers, these were bare. He put his finger to his lips to indicate they should make as little noise as possible. They climbed down three flights before he stopped on a landing and opened another door. This led to a hallway vibrating with the hum of whatever machinery kept going when the ship was docked.

Chet stopped and unbuckled the belt of his uniform to let the pants drop to the floor, pulling off his shirt at the same time. Underneath he was wearing the same style jumpsuit and vest he'd given Nicole. Once again, the sleeves and pants were too short. He stuffed the ship's uniform into a nearby trash bin, then turned to open another door, this one leading outside. The moment he did, a chill wind whipped in, carrying spray from the river. Chet reached out to grab the ladder attached to the side of the boat. He swung onto it, descending a few steps before beckoning Nicole to follow.

She looked down. In the river, perhaps twenty feet below, was a rowboat with two men inside. She tried to grab the ladder as Chet had done, but it was out of reach. She screwed up her courage and leaned much farther out, hanging onto the doorframe with one hand and grabbing a rung of the ladder with the other. When she let go of the doorframe, she was able to grasp the ladder with both hands. But that was as far as she got. She didn't have enough strength in her arms to swing around and place her feet on one of the rungs. Chet reached up and grabbed her around the middle. He held on until she was safely mounted on the ladder. He started climbing down, and she followed, her fear of falling somewhat mitigated by the sight of this big man just below, ready to catch her.

At the bottom, Chet swung himself to the side so Nicole could get in the boat first. It teetered as she stepped in and sat down, then rocked wildly when Chet got in and settled next to her.

"Let's go," he whispered.

The two men sitting in the front of the boat started rowing. They passed dozens of sleeping tour ships, which stretched a good quarter mile along the dock. When they passed the last one, the rowers turned the boat toward the shore, which was reinforced with a tall, concrete sea wall. It had a ladder attached, similar to the one on the side of the ship, except this one was much taller, reaching to the top of the wall.

Chet pointed to the ladder then up, indicating they were going to climb it. She wasn't sure she could make it, but she climbed on and gamely started up. Chet followed close behind while the oarsmen remained in the boat. Nicole was almost halfway up when she stopped and looked down at Chet.

"Wait! My arms are giving out. I've got to stop a few minutes and rest."

He moved up behind her. "Do I have permission to pick you up?"

"OK," she said.

He balanced on the step, freeing his hands to turn her and position her against his chest and shoulder. "You all right?" he said. "I'll be using my arms on the ladder, so you'll have to hold onto me with your arms and legs. He waited for her to wrap her legs around his middle, her arms around his neck. The position was awkward and, at the same time, oddly comforting. His body was warm and formed a barrier against the bitter wind.

"All right?" he said.

"All right." Looking down over his shoulder, she could see the rowboat getting smaller, the water farther away. It started to make her dizzy, so she closed her eyes. When they reached the top, he put her down. They were in a narrow space outside the embankment's safety fence. Chet jumped it, one hand on the rail before helping her over.

A motorcycle was parked there, with two helmets hanging from the handlebars. Chet handed Nicole one and put on the other. They climbed on the bike, and he took off without turning on his headlight. They left the embankment to ride through the streets. They rode a good while before he stopped and parked the motorcycle behind a large trash bin in an alley.

"We walk the rest of the way," he said. "I'm afraid you'll have to leave your coat here. Sorry about that. I know how cold it is."

As Nicole handed Chet the coat, she noticed he wasn't wearing anything over his worker's outfit, even though the wind had been bitterly cold on the water and when they were climbing the wall. Apparently, the cold didn't make his bones ache the way it did hers. Draping her coat over his arm, he took the bike helmets and hung them back on the handlebars. He opened the storage compartment behind the seat of the motorcycle, pulled out two red construction helmets, and put her coat inside.

They walked for about twenty minutes. Neither spoke. Nicole was uncomfortable with the silence, but she knew he wouldn't answer the questions she was dying to ask. Who was he? Where had he grown up? How long had he been a spy? Had he always wanted to do this or was it something he happened into? Was he married? Did his wife know what he did for a living? Even more important, she wanted to ask if he knew Reinhardt and had any idea what had happened to him. Aside from this, she couldn't imagine what they'd talk about. He seemed like the kind of man who didn't have much use for small talk, or talking at all, if he could avoid it.

At last she spotted Red Square in the distance, well-lit and easily recognizable by the colorful onion domes of the cathedral. When they arrived, three guards with automatic weapons were stationed at the entrance, which was blocked off with traffic barriers.

"Stay behind me," Chet instructed. "Let me do the talking and try not to call attention to yourself." She followed slightly behind him as he approached the guard who seemed to be in charge, the only one in a police uniform.

Chet pulled a paper from his pocket and handed it to the guard, speaking to him in Russian. Nicole was surprised but only for a moment. Since Chet was a British spy working in Russia, of course he'd speak the language. The exchange with the guard was brief. He handed the paper back and waved them in, pushing aside one of the traffic barriers in front of the gate. Chet was now walking slightly behind Nicole, keeping her out of the guards' sight. Only now did she realize what a problem her size was. They'd never employ a five-feet-one lightweight for the physical demands of construction work.

Tonight the workers were concentrated at the far end, where they were putting the finishing touches on bleachers that were almost complete. This area was lit by powerful lights sitting on the cobblestone pavement. The rest of the square was in deep shadow. A couple of guards seemed to be patrolling the perimeter. At the moment, the guards were on the opposite side of the square from Chet and Nicole. The rest of the security crew seemed to be stationed at the square's many entrances, where blockades had been set up to keep people out. For the moment, the rest of the unfinished bleachers and the grandstand were deserted and unlit except for the glow reflecting from the spotlights.

"All right, now show me where it is," Chet said.

Nicole led him to the front of the grandstand, went around to the side, and lifted the heavy draped fabric covering the area underneath. He followed her into the pitch dark of the stand's underside. As soon as they were both in, he pulled a flashlight out of his pocket and clicked it on. The beam wandered along the inner supports until it rested on the opposite side where something covered with a tarp formed an uneven pyramid. They both headed toward it. Chet lifted the tarp, revealing a pile of cinderblocks, one on top of the other. On the ground in front of it was a metal toolbox. Chet leaned in close to examine it. Nicole did the same. Three cables extended from the back of the box, running under the pyramid of blocks. Nicole backed off when Chet got on his hands and knees and lowered his head to listen.

"Is it ticking?" Nicole said.

Chet looked up quickly as if he'd forgotten she was there. He held his finger to his lips to shush her and shook his head. He stood, covered the blocks with the tarp, and the beam of his flashlight led them back to where they'd entered. He stuck his head out to make sure it was safe to leave then beckoned Nicole to follow. He led her toward the wall in back of the grandstand.

About a dozen steps ahead of her, he reached the rear of the grandstand and was about to turn and disappear behind it when a voice rang out "*Stoy!*" Chet waved Nicole back and started to run. She slunk into the shadows. Two guards, shouting for him to stop, were in close pursuit. As they ran, a shot rang out and, after a few seconds, two more. She could hear running footsteps getting fainter until they faded completely.

Nicole hoped this meant he'd gotten away, but she had no way of knowing. She decided not to follow the route he'd taken along the back of the grandstand. If it wasn't closely watched before, it would be now. She returned to the square, wondering what to do. It would be impossible to leave by any route other than the one she and Chet had entered. All the other exits were barricaded and guarded. She headed toward the front entrance, sticking to the shadows.

The guards were still stationed outside. She waited a good ten minutes before a group of a dozen workers came along, apparently finished for the night and intending to leave by the front gate. She attached herself to them, taking long strides to keep up. When they reached the street, she slipped into the grounds of a large building and waited for her companions to disappear down the road before turning and making a wide detour around Red Square's entrance. She headed back the way she and Chet had come.

She normally had a good sense of direction, but in this foreign city, in the middle of the night, she wasn't sure she could find her way back to the motorcycle. The streets, filled with office buildings, were deserted. They looked familiar only in the sense that, with a few exceptions, they all looked alike. She kept going, convinced she was lost until she spotted the alley with the trash bin. The motorcycle was still there, helmets dangling from the handlebars. Chet hadn't told her what to do if they ran into trouble, but it made sense to return to this spot. If he escaped, he'd come here. If not, she'd wait until morning and take a cab back to the ship.

She got her coat out of the bike's storage compartment and put it on. She sent an urgent message through her new watch, explaining that they'd run into trouble leaving Red Square. The watch didn't flash when she was done the way her other one had. She wondered if the message had been received. But this watch was a completely different model. Perhaps it didn't have that feature.

She was shaking and not just from the cold. She was terrified that Chet might be bleeding to death on the street somewhere. One thing she knew beyond all doubt: explosives had been planted beneath the speakers' stand in Red Square, and someone had to disarm them before Victory Day, which was only four days away.

Suddenly, Chet appeared, running at top speed. He didn't seem surprised to see her. As he hopped on the motorcycle, his breath was coming in short gasps.

"Get on," he said, tossing aside the helmets hanging from the handlebar. Nicole climbed on and wrapped her arms around him. "Let me know if you see a black car," he said as the bike roared to life.

They'd just gone a short distance when a black car came careening around a corner several blocks behind them. "I think that's them," Nicole said. Chet took a quick turn onto a cross street, skidding across a public square.

The black car followed. The motorcycle was still in motion when gun shots rang out. The bike stopped abruptly, causing Nicole to tumble off and land painfully on the cement. Chet planted his feet on the ground and stood there a moment before collapsing. Both he and the motorcycle landed on the pavement. The car's doors slammed as two men got out. Nicole, her body protesting, rolled sideways. She managed to crawl behind a statue of a man on a horse. She peeked around it and watched the men approach Chet. They bent over him and exchanged comments, probably discussing whether he might be still alive. One of them knelt down and passed his hand over Chet's face to see if he was breathing. He stood up and shook his head. The pair walked back to their car and drove off.

As soon as they were out of sight, Nicole hurried over to Chet. She placed her hand on his carotid artery but couldn't find a pulse. She'd almost given up when she felt it, so faint it was barely detectable. She checked to see where he'd been shot. The side of his jumpsuit was soaked with blood. She located the source and tried to remember what her first aid class had taught her about pressure points. She decided where the best spot might be and pressed it with one hand while awkwardly fumbling through his pockets with the other. She located a phone and pulled it out. It took her a moment to remember that 103 was the Russian equivalent of 911. She punched in the numbers. While it rang, she tucked the phone under her chin so she could put pressure on Chet's wound with both hands.

When the operator answered in Russian, Nicole kept repeating the word *English* until someone came on with a rudimentary command of the language.

"Name?" he said.

"Sally Holmes" was the first thing that came to her, the name of the rose in a container on her condo's balcony. When he asked for the location of the victim, she looked around. No street name was in sight, but a distinctive-looking building across the street—a two-story brick with ornately decorated arched windows—was flying the French flag.

She made an educated guess. "He's in front of the building across from the French Embassy." When she was sure the person on the other end understood, she let the phone drop onto the pavement and waited—still pressing Chet's wound—until she heard a siren. As it approached, she got up and, ignoring the pain of her bruises and scraped knees, dashed for a stairwell that led to a basement entrance of the building behind them. She climbed far enough down to be of sight but still able to rise on her toes and see what was happening. She prayed the paramedics had gotten to him in time and that they were halfway competent.

She regretted leaving the burner phone behind. That had been a mistake. Kolkov had her phone, and she knew she'd be needing one soon.

The ambulance came, and the paramedics loaded Chet inside. One of them spotted the phone lying on the pavement and picked it up. She was relieved when they hooked Chet up to a drip. That meant he was still holding on. Maybe they could save him.

It was freezing in the stairwell. She tried to send another message with her watch, but it seemed completely dead this time. Then she remembered falling off the motorcycle. The impact must have broken it. There was nothing she could do but wait, shivering, until the first hint of dawn. As soon as it was barely light, she walked back toward Red Square. She didn't have to go far before she was able to flag down a cab.

When she arrived at *Queen of the Volga*, it was early. Fortunately, access through the other ships was already open. Her coat had splotches of Chet's blood on it, but no one seemed to notice or care. She went immediately to her suite. Still shivering from the cold, she took off the ruined coat and put it in the hamper. Only then did she look at the watch. Sure enough, the crystal was shattered and a piece was missing. The watch said 2:00 a.m., but the clock on the credenza said it was 6:30.

With her watch broken, how would she get in touch with

Chet's team to let them know what had happened? Even if he pulled through and regained consciousness, he'd be stuck in the hospital. It was unlikely he'd have the means of contacting his people.

Still considering what to do, she took off all the layers of clothes and stepped into a hot shower, attempting to get warm. She changed into her pj's, wrapped herself in the terry robe, and—still as cold as when she walked in—climbed into bed.

After the night's misadventure, her thoughts were on Chet, his cool in the face of any situation thrown at him—until that bullet found him. She wondered if he was fatalistic about his work. Had he been willing to die for his country? Or did he believe himself invincible? She remembered all the questions that went through her head as they walked to Red Square. She wished she hadn't been too intimidated by him to ask.

She remembered the arrangements that were being made to extract her from Russia. But there was no way for anyone to let her know about them now that the watch was broken. She felt a tug in her gut, the feeling that something even worse was about to happen. She had to let someone know about the explosives and where they were hidden. But who? She'd been warned not to tell the Russian police. If only Chet had given her a number to call if things went sideways.

She had only three more days to find someone who could help clean up the situation in Red Square. She vibrated with adrenalin, certain she'd never be able to sleep. But, against all logic, she sank into a deep, dreamless sleep almost as soon as she tucked the duvet under her chin.

The midday sun was shining through her porthole when she was startled awake. Someone was banging on her door. "Police! Open up!" Kolkov was back. She hadn't escaped him after all.

CHAPTER SEVEN

WHEN NICOLE OPENED THE DOOR, Kolkov was even more abrupt than on his previous visit. No greeting, just, "Get dressed. I take you in for questioning." He talked fast, radiating impatience.

"Why can't we do it here like before?" Nicole said.

"Get dressed!" he shouted, pointing to the bedroom. "I give five minutes."

She went to her room and got out a black turtleneck, tan slacks, and her boots before heading into the bathroom.

Kolkov was waiting at the door and seemed to be in a tremendous hurry. As she approached, he stepped toward her and firmly gripped her by the arm as if he expected her to try to escape.

She pulled back, pointing to the closet. "I have to get my jacket."

He let go so she could pull out her zippered hoody and put it on. It was going to be cold out. She longed for her warm coat, but it was in the hamper, stained with Chet's blood—something else to worry about if Kolkov decided to search the cabin again. She grabbed her purse as Kolkov pulled her out the door.

Other passengers stared as Kolkov led Nicole down to the main deck and across the ramp to the ship next to theirs. Surely they could tell she was being taken from the ship involuntarily; perhaps they recognized Kolkov from his previous visit. But no one stepped forward to ask what was happening. Nicole wondered what they were thinking.

The pair of them drew an even larger audience as they walked through the four vessels anchored between *Queen of the Volga* and the dock. Finally, they reached the street, where a boxy black sedan was standing at the curb with a uniformed policeman at the wheel. Kolkov put Nicole in back, not relaxing his hold on her until he was about to close the door. He climbed in the front seat, and they took off.

Traffic was heavy, and it took a while to get to their destination: an imposing, gray office building with no identifying sign in front. It bore no resemblance to the sprawling Moscow Police headquarters Nicole had seen on her bus tour of the city.

Without explanation, she was marched inside. In the lobby, they passed through a gauntlet of security checks, including a pat down by a male guard who wore an infuriating smirk while he searched her. As they headed into the building's main corridor, she looked around, taking note of her surroundings. Since she wasn't being arrested—at least that was what Kolkov had said— she had no reason to look for an escape route. On the other hand, she had the feeling the situation was still evolving. She'd expected Kolkov to take her to a police station, but this was no police station. It had the look of a government building filled with high-placed officials. Gold Cyrillic lettering appeared on the doors along the wood-paneled corridor. The floor was highly polished marble.

They took an elevator to the top floor and walked down a long hallway. Kolkov stopped at a pair of double doors marked with more rows of lettering than appeared elsewhere. It also bore the crest of the Russian Federation, with its double-headed eagle. Before entering, Kolkov took off his hat. Inside, a woman sat at a desk facing the door. She was wearing a boxy brown suit that looked like a leftover from the Soviet era. Her gray hair was pulled back tight into an oversized bun. She and Kolkov spoke in Russian. From the way the two kept glancing at Nicole, it was clear they were discussing her. At last, the woman picked up the phone, spoke a few words, then addressed Kolkov again, apparently telling him to go into the office.

"You come," he said to Nicole. When he took hold of her arm, she noticed he was trembling. *Why is he afraid?* Nicole thought. *Whoever's in this office must have a great deal of power over him.* Kolkov gave two light raps on the door. A man's voice called from inside, and Kolkov led Nicole into a large corner office with a view of the city. The room was nicely appointed with a large walnut desk, where a man in his late fifties was seated. He wore wire-rimmed glasses and was completely bald, his head so shiny it looked as if he'd polished it. He and Kolkov exchanged a few words, after which Kolkov left. Nicole noted that he backed his way to the door, as if leaving a royal presence.

The man stood up. "Please, have a seat. I think the blue one on the left is the most comfortable." His English was excellent with hardly a trace of an accent, his tone cordial, even friendly. Nicole sat on the chair he'd indicated. It was beyond her to figure out what was going on. Was this man, who appeared to be a high-level bureaucrat, playing good cop to Kolkov's bad cop?

"Let me introduce myself. I'm Sergey Tarasov, deputy minister of internal affairs for the Russian Federation. And—for the record—you are?"

"Nicole Graves. I'm an American citizen. I'm here as a tourist on a riverboat cruise to St. Petersburg."

"And your occupation?"

"I'm a private investigator, but I'm not working at present. I'm on vacation."

"I understand. And I want to apologize for interrupting your holiday. You see, this unfortunate death of a foreign tourist on a Russian cruise ship has caught attention at the highest levels of our government. That's why I'm interviewing you today instead of the police. I notice that on your visa, you identified yourself as an office worker. Why didn't you state that you're a private investigator?"

Nicole paused to consider how to respond. She wasn't the one who'd applied for the visa. It was British intelligence. "I used to put that on my visas when I traveled abroad," she finally said. "But immigration officials would take me aside and question me at length. They seemed to think I was in their country for something other than tourism. It was a waste of everyone's time. I'm just another tourist on vacation. My occupation is irrelevant."

"I agree, although immigration officials do have the right to know who is visiting their country. But this isn't germane to today's business. You are not suspected of any wrongdoing, though we do believe you may have witnessed something that would help us solve the murder on the ship. I also want to ask about your friendship with a Ukrainian national named Darina Kravchenko, who is presently under arrest."

"Darina Kravchenko?" Nicole felt a wave of relief. This explained everything. It was all a misunderstanding. "You've made a mistake. I don't know anyone by that name."

"I'm afraid you do, Ms. Graves, although you may not be aware of it. You see, Ms. Kravchenko uses many aliases. One of them is Katarina, or Kat, Heikkinen. I understand that you spent a great deal of time with her on this tour. When did you meet? What were the circumstances?"

Nicole thought about his question, which had been asked in the mildest of tone as if he were merely curious, not an official interviewing a murder witness. "All right," she said. "But first I want to know why you arrested Kat. What is she charged with?"

"Why, I thought you knew. She's been charged with the murder of Derek Swan."

Nicole blinked. A long moment passed before she recovered

from her surprise. Whatever Kat was guilty of, it wasn't murder.

"How would that be possible?" she said. "I saw Swan's body after they pulled him out. He was big, maybe 250 pounds. It would have taken a couple of strong men to lift him over the rail and into the water."

"Obviously, she would have needed help," he said. "Or else she hired people to take care of it. There's no doubt about it. She's already admitted her guilt, but she refuses to tell us anything more. We're hoping you can give us a description of the people who threw Mr. Swan overboard."

"I didn't see them."

He sighed. "I'm afraid you're not telling the truth. The ship has a surveillance camera that caught you standing on the deck around the time of the murder, facing the spot where it took place. Unfortunately, no camera was positioned to catch the crime itself."

She opened her mouth to speak, then closed it again.

"Do you still deny you saw anything?"

Her face grew hot. He'd caught her in a lie. What could she say that wouldn't make things worse?

"This is crazy. I have a right to a phone call. I want to speak to the American Embassy."

"I'm afraid such calls are reserved for people who've been arrested. And, by the way—" A tone of sarcasm had crept into his voice. "Your embassy doesn't intervene in Russian police matters involving American citizens. But let me reiterate: no one is planning to arrest you. When we do arrest an American citizen, it can become an international incident. In this case, it's not worth the furor it would stir up. All we want is a description of the murderers."

She seized on a reply she hoped would sound reasonable. "That's why I didn't report it," she said. "I can't give you a description. I saw three figures by the ship's railing as I walked by, but they were turned away from me, and I couldn't see their faces. And I didn't see Mr. Swan thrown off the ship. That must have happened after I started back up to my cabin. When I heard him scream, I turned around and hurried back to the main deck. That's when I heard passengers saying someone had gone overboard. I suspected it might have had something to do with those people I passed. But I didn't mention it because I knew this would happen." She held up her hands in a gesture of frustration. "I didn't want to get involved because I really didn't see anything, and I knew it would turn into a hassle if I spoke up. The only time I got a good look at Swan was after the divers brought him up, and he was lying on the deck."

"All right. Maybe you can help us in some other way. Let's start at the beginning. How did you meet Ms. Kravchenko—or Kat, as you call her—and what was your relationship with her?"

Nicole swallowed hard, surprised that Tarasov was willing to accept her denial so easily. Was he planning to circle back to it later? She had no reason to trust this man with his perfect English and good manners. But after a moment's thought, she decided she could tell most of what she knew about Kat without giving away the information she'd promised not to reveal.

"OK, I'll tell you, but I really can't see how any of it is relevant. I met Kat at dinner on the first full day of the tour," she said. "She approached my table, introduced herself, and asked if she could sit with me. I preferred sitting alone, but I didn't want to be rude, so I said yes."

"Ah-h. And what did you talk about?"

"She did most of the talking, mainly gossip about other passengers she'd met at lunch."

"The two of you were constantly together the last few days. You must have enjoyed her company."

"At first. But then she wanted to spend every minute with me, and I need time to myself. I also wanted a chance to mingle with the other passengers, so this became a problem. On the third day of the tour, I managed to sneak away from her and spend some time on my own."

"She must have talked about more than this common gossip you mention." His tone had turned less conciliatory. "I know how women talk, confide in each other."

"Well, there was a little more, but I don't see how—" Her voice trailed off. She might as well repeat what Kat had said, even though it was probably a pack of lies. "All right. She told me this trip was supposed to be her honeymoon, but her fiancé backed out of the wedding at the last minute. She seemed to be quite broken up about it. She also mentioned that she was a financial manager at a large bank in Manhattan, although she didn't say which one. Oh, and she grew up in Switzerland and, after her parents' divorce, divided her time between New York and Geneva."

"These are all lies, things she made up to give herself a credible background outside Ukraine." He paused, then added. "You're a smart woman. You know the kind of thing we're looking for. She conspired with others to murder someone, and we want to know who they are and why this man was killed."

"Well, she certainly didn't tell me anything about it. If she actually did such a terrible thing, why would she confide in me?"

"Come now," he said. "She must have dropped a hint about what she was up to. You had several days to observe her and listen to what she had to say. We want to know why she was on that ship and what her relationship was with Mr. Swan. Any information of that nature would help us find the killers. And it would help you."

Nicole's uneasiness grew. "What do you mean it would help me?"

"Until we're satisfied you've told us everything, we can't allow you to leave Moscow."

"But that's all I know. Kat and I talked about trivial things—

fashion, books, movies, other passengers. She didn't mention anything that suggested she even knew the murder victim." Nicole was briefly silent as she remembered one of her first conversations with Kat. "She told me she'd boarded the ship the morning after the murder and had missed the visit from the police."

"Another of her lies," he said. "We have irrefutable proof that she was on board at the time of the murder. What else did she say? Did she tell you why she'd come to Moscow? What her plans were?"

"I told you. She said she was on the trip because it was supposed to be her honeymoon and was already paid for when her fiancé cancelled the wedding. From what she told me, her only plan was to visit tourist sites on the cruise from Moscow to St. Petersburg."

Once more, he sighed. "That's simply not good enough. I want you to think this over carefully. I believe you know more, perhaps a lot more. There's still time if you choose to cooperate. When your ship leaves Moscow tonight, you could be on it."

"Honestly, I've already told you everything." A pleading tone had entered her voice; she was starting to be genuinely alarmed. "If the ship leaves without me, what about the clothes I left on the ship, my bags—my passport? And I have nowhere to stay in Moscow, or are you planning to put me in jail to try and sweat me for information I don't have?"

"Don't be so melodramatic." Tarasov was clearly losing his patience. "We'll arrange accommodations at the Tourist Hotel— not as luxurious as your suite on the ship I'm afraid. The police will pack the things you left behind and deliver them to your hotel. Except for your passport, of course. We'll keep it for the time being."

He stood and resumed the polite demeanor he'd shown when she first walked in. "Again, I'm sorry for the inconvenience. I truly hope you'll remember something that can help us so you can quickly rejoin your shipmates." He smiled as he reached under his desk, presumably pushing a button to summon his secretary. The door opened, and she appeared.

"Take her to Colonel Kolkov,"

"Of course," the secretary said. "He's just outside."

Kolkov delivered her back to the car, firmly holding onto her until she was seated inside. They drove to an old five-story brick building with a big rooftop sign that read *"Турист"* in roman letters, then lower down, something in Cyrillic. It was one of several brick buildings in a cluster, all in the same state of disrepair. Nicole assumed *турист* was the Russian word for tourist. At first, she thought Tarasov had meant it was tourist class. As it turned out, *tourist* was both the name and class of the hotel, which was quite a few rungs below the places where Nicole usually stayed and light years below her accommodations on the ship.

Kolkov marched her into the lobby and stood back as the woman at the desk shoved the credit card reader across the counter to Nicole, indicating she was to produce a credit card. Nicole reached into her purse and handed over the card. An impression of it was taken, and she signed the receipt, although she couldn't read it and had no idea what the room charge would be. From the depressed condition of the lobby, she couldn't imagine it would be much.

The woman spoke at length in Russian, giving what sounded like detailed instructions for Nicole to find her room, ignoring her protestations that she didn't speak the language. Nicole glanced over at Kolkov, who appeared deep in thought. As the desk clerk wound down, she handed Nicole a map showing five buildings that apparently housed the hotel complex. The clerk pointed to one building and said, "Bot." She then circled the building with her pen and wrote "516" in the margin. She handed Nicole a large, old-fashioned key and pointed toward the exit.

As she headed outside, Kolkov followed. He accompanied her to another building where a uniformed policeman was waiting. Without a word, Kolkov walked away, leaving the uniformed cop to accompany her inside. He was a large man with a fringe of brown hair and sleepy eyes.

The building had no reception area, just a bleak entry hall with two elevators. One appeared to be stuck on the fifth floor. She and the cop waited while the other car slowly made its way down to the lobby. It was tiny, barely big enough for the two of them to squeeze in.

The policeman got off with her on the fifth floor and trailed after her. The dimly lit hallway smelled of mothballs and disinfectant. When she reached room 516, she had a hard time getting the key to turn, struggling until it grudgingly clicked and the door swung open. She hurried inside and locked the door. The cop could hang around all day, but at least she had the room to herself.

It was tiny, furnished with the bare minimum: a bed that sagged in the middle, a bureau topped with an oval mirror, and an overstuffed red velour chair that appeared to be the only recent addition. The red stood out garishly in contrast to the rest of the decor, which was in faded browns and beiges. There was no TV. The bathroom was white with old-fashioned black and white mosaic tiles on the floor. It appeared reasonably clean.

After looking around, she noticed a phone on top of the bureau. If she could make herself understood, maybe the desk clerk would connect her with the U.S. Embassy. Tarasov had said they wouldn't help in a situation like this, but surely they could do something. She picked up the receiver and put it to her ear. It was silent, without a dial tone. The phone was out of order or had been deliberately shut off.

She hung up and went over to the window to see if this might be a means of escape. It was a clear drop, five floors straight down. The view was even more depressing than the room. It took in a decommissioned railway yard with a few derelict trains that might have been used decades ago to transport prisoners to Siberia.

Just then, someone knocked at the door. When she opened it, the policeman who'd followed her stepped inside. He had her suitcases, and she wondered where he'd gotten them since he hadn't been carrying them earlier. Perhaps someone had just delivered them and brought them up in the elevator. Wordlessly, he set them down, gave a slight dip of his head to acknowledge her, and left, closing the door behind him. To her alarm, she heard a key turn in the lock. She tried the door. It was locked.

For God's sake, she thought. She got out the key the hotel clerk had given her, but it wouldn't go in. She bent down to look in the keyhole. Something had been put inside, blocking her key. The policeman must have done this to make sure she couldn't leave. She banged on the door and shouted, "Let me out. The door is stuck!"

Something rattled on the other side of the door, then a key turned in the lock. The same policeman appeared. "Da?" he said. She noticed a chair in the hallway outside her door. He'd been sitting there to make sure she didn't leave.

"Why did you lock my door?" she demanded. "I need to get something to eat." Assuming he didn't understand English, she mimed holding a plate in one hand and lifting a fork to her mouth with the other.

What he understood was that she wanted to leave. He shook his finger at her and came out with a heavily accented "You stay" before firmly closing the door and locking it.

She went over to the window again and gazed out. The window was dirty, inside and out. A large decal in one corner showed a picture of a wine bottle overlaid by a red circle with a forward slash through the middle. She took this to mean guests were not allowed to throw bottles out the window. Did people actually do that? The decal reminded her she was thirsty as well as hungry. Was it possible this dump had a minibar? She wanted a cold drink or maybe even a glass of wine.

She gave the room another look, but there was no minibar. The bathroom had a faucet but no glasses to drink from, nor was there any bottled water. She put her face next to the faucet and sucked in a long drink.

She looked at her wrist, expecting to see the watch so she could check for messages. Only then did she remember the watch was broken, zipped into a compartment of her purse. For the first time since Kolkov had knocked on her door, she thought of Chet. She still hadn't been able to let his team know that he'd been badly injured, much less give them the location of the explosives. That was completely out of the question now that she was a prisoner here.

She'd missed breakfast and now lunchtime had passed as well. As the afternoon dragged on, she banged on the door repeatedly, demanding food, using every synonym for the word she could think of in case the policeman knew one of them and would realize she was asking for something other than to be allowed to leave. There was no response, and she began to wonder if he was still out there. She tried her key again. This finally got a response from her guard, who loudly thumped on the door and shouted a command in Russian she could tell was some kind of rebuke.

It was getting dark outside when the policeman finally opened the door and handed her a tray holding a mug and a covered dish. Nicole took it and, having nowhere else to put it, set it on the bed. The dish held some kind of meat patty with dumplings. It didn't look bad, although it didn't smell much like food. She tasted it. The meat had an odd, chemical taste that made her wonder what was in it. The dumplings were surprisingly tough, the brown gravy tasteless. The mug of coffee was tepid but otherwise not too bad. She drank it down and put the mug in her bathroom for later use.

She picked up the tray and knocked on the door to let the policeman know he could take it away. Getting no response, she banged harder. Maybe he'd left his post for a break or to use the men's room. In an old structure like this, she was pretty sure he'd have to go down to the first floor or even leave the premises.

She continued banging on the door until a woman's voice said, "Da?"

Nicole called out that the door was stuck, demonstrating by rattling the doorknob until door shook. When she heard the maid jiggling the lock, Nicole rushed into the bathroom, plugged the sink and turned on the water full force. When she returned to the door, the woman was still struggling with the lock. Nicole prayed she'd be able to get it open before the policeman returned. At last the maid managed to remove whatever was blocking the key and opened the door.

Nicole touched the woman's arm and pointed toward bathroom where the sound of running water was accompanied by the sink's overflow splashing onto the floor. As the maid disappeared into the bathroom, Nicole picked up her purse and jacket and walked out the door. She spotted a sign at the end of the hall with the universal symbols of exit: an arrow and a flight of stairs. She started to run.

CHAPTER EIGHT

NICOLE RAN DOWN THREE FLIGHTS OF STAIRS. When she reached the hotel's second-floor landing, she heard a door above slam shut and heavy footsteps hurrying down. The policeman must have arrived back in time to see her leave and was coming after her. It occurred to her that if he'd called for backup, she might emerge onto the street and find the police waiting for her there. Instead of continuing down, she opened the door to the second floor and silently closed it behind her.

At the end of a long corridor, she spotted a lit green-and-white sign with a word in Cyrillic that she took to mean *exit*. Without pausing, she ran for the door nearest the sign. It opened onto a dimly lit stairwell. Judging by the dust and spiderwebs, these stairs had fallen out of use long ago, perhaps when the elevators were installed. They were constructed of wooden slats, several broken or missing. The first step creaked and sunk a bit as she put her weight on it, which made her slow down and proceed with caution.

At the bottom, she opened the door and found herself in a large room. Above a door in the corner was another exit sign. The room was filled with clothing racks. The one nearest the exit was jammed with coats, jackets, and other apparel that appeared to belong to the help. The others were filled with hotel uniforms— blue maid's dresses and matching coveralls for maintenance workers. She quickly went through the coat rack, looking for something to change her appearance as well as protect her from the cold night air. She found a brown, full-length coat with a fleece lining that looked as if it would do the job. After putting it on, she turned to look in a large, free-standing mirror. The coat was several sizes too big and visibly frayed on the sleeve cuffs and around the collar. She turned away from the mirror, reminding herself this was no time for vanity. She hung the sweatshirt hoodie she'd been wearing where the coat had been before something occurred to her. Her lightweight jacket was no substitute for this warm coat. Whoever owned it was going to be cold and might not have money for new outerwear. She got out her wallet and, after a quick calculation, stuffed a 5,000 ruble note into the sweatshirt pocket. This taken care of, she headed for the exit.

Outside, she found herself in an alley populated with overflowing trash bins that gave off a powerful smell, as if the garbage hadn't been picked up in weeks. She followed the alley for several blocks, passing more overfilled garbage containers before exiting onto a boulevard in a business area. Three- and four-story buildings lined the street with shops and restaurants at ground level and what looked like offices above. Nearing the end of rush hour, there was plenty of foot traffic.

She took a deep breath to calm herself and slowed her pace, hoping to fit in with the flow of pedestrians. Meanwhile, she kept watch for American or British tourists. She needed to find someone who could speak English and might be willing to lend her a phone.

Glancing in the windows she passed, she could see that shops in this neighborhood weren't upscale enough to attract many tourists. Most were selling newspapers and packaged junk food. She kept an eye out for a place to buy a burner phone, but none seemed to be on offer. Some shops featured signs with graphics— sometimes hand-drawn—offering currency exchange and check cashing services. Tiny grocery stores tried to lure customers in with produce displayed in crates on the sidewalk. Hardware stores had windows filled with brooms, mops, and cleaning supplies. A small number of marginal businesses were selling assorted odds and ends, new and used.

She came to a women's clothing store—an anomaly in this neighborhood—and stopped to look at the display. The clothes were reasonably fashionable, but the uneven way they hung on the mannequins suggested they were poorly made of cheap fabric. When she saw her reflection in the window, she remembered that she wasn't exactly presentable. How likely was it a shop owner would welcome her in and let her use the phone? Maybe it would improve her chances if she made a purchase before she asked.

She turned away from the passersby and checked her wallet to see how much money she had left. She was pleased to find over 3,500 rubles, worth almost fifty dollars. In addition, she had a one-hundred-dollar bill she always kept for emergencies in the hidden pocket of her wallet. If she changed that into rubles, it would keep her going for a few days. For the moment, she took out a 1000 ruble note and put it in her coat pocket, then zipped her wallet back into her purse.

Nicole entered the shop, giving the saleswoman her most confident smile. "Do you speak English?"

"Yezz." Instead of smiling back, the woman frowned. Only then did Nicole remember the tour guide's warning that, here in Russia, a smile from a stranger might be considered an insult. The woman coolly sized Nicole up from head to toe, then looked away.

Nicole went up to a counter with a display of necklaces and earrings. The woman hurried over as if she thought Nicole might be planning to steal a piece of jewelry or perhaps scoop the entire display into her purse and run off.

"How much is this one?" Nicole pointed at a silver necklace with a blue stone surrounded by sparkly diamond-like chips.

"7,500 rubles."

"Really?" Nicole did a quick calculation. That amounted to more than a hundred dollars. She didn't have that much in rubles. Besides, the necklace looked like cheap costume jewelry, worth about twenty bucks back home, if that much. She pointed to a plainer necklace, silver with a small mother-of-pearl pendant.

"Is 7,500 rubles," the saleswoman said. "All same price. You serious buyer? If not, you must leave. I can't spend all day watching customer."

Despite the woman's rudeness, Nicole decided to push ahead. She pulled out the 1,000 ruble note. "May I use your phone? I have money. I'll gladly pay for the call."

"No phone," the woman said, although there was one sitting on a cabinet behind her. "Customers not allowed. You leave now."

Nicole did as she was told. Back on the sidewalk, she soon found herself walking behind two well-dressed boys in their early teens who were obviously tourists. One of them was wearing a pair of AirPods sticking straight up, making him look like a visitor from outer space. The boys were speaking French peppered with English phrases. She hurried to catch up with them.

"Excuse me," she said. "Someone stole my cell phone and passport. I need to call the American Embassy. Would you lend me your phone? I'll pay you." She pulled the 1,000 ruble note out of her pocket.

The boys stared at her. The one without the AirPods started talking to the other boy in French, apparently translating what she'd just said. They stepped to the side so they weren't holding up pedestrians while the boy with the AirPods dug in his pocket, pulled out a cell phone, and gave it to her.

"Merci," she said, handing him the 1,000 ruble note. Only then did she realize she didn't have a number for the embassy. She dug through her purse for her tourist's guide and thumbed through until she found the number. She tapped the cell to wake it, only to be greeted by a demand for a passcode. She handed it to the boy. He at once saw her problem and typed something in. She took it back and had just entered the embassy's number when she noticed a squad car pull up to a nearby curb. Two policemen got out and, after looking around, headed in her direction. She turned and started to run.

The boys were in close pursuit, shouting, "*Au voleur!*" People stopped, curious about the scene, but no one joined the chase. Perhaps they didn't know the French phrase for *stop thief*; perhaps they didn't care. Nicole wanted to return the phone, but she didn't dare slow down to hand it over. Instead, she tossed it back over her shoulder, hoping the boys would be able to catch it. There was a cracking sound as the phone hit the pavement. She could hear the boys shouting after her. She'd taken French in school but had no idea what they were saying. She had a hunch those words wouldn't have been taught in class.

She turned at the next corner, where a throng of people were gathered. She hoped to get lost in the crowd and slip away by a side street, but it turned out to be a broad stone-paved plaza that dead-ended into the backs of several office buildings. The only way out was the way she'd come in. In the plaza, food venders were selling their wares, and the crowd was watching two buskers performing an elaborate juggling act.

Three office buildings had their back entrances here. Nicole figured they'd probably be locked at this hour but rushed over to the nearest one. As she drew close, she couldn't believe her luck. The door was propped open with a rubber doorstop, allowing access to anyone who wanted to enter. As she slipped inside, she kicked the doorstop out of the way and let the door close. The doorknob inside didn't seem to have a way to lock it, but since it had been propped open, she was pretty sure it automatically locked itself. She leaned against it, trying to catch her breath, then froze when the doorknob rattled as someone tried to get in.

She had no doubt it was the police, who were soon shouting and pounding on the door. At last the banging stopped, and she could hear the murmur of conversation, growing fainter as they walked away. Had they given up or were they heading around the block to the building's front entrance to continue pursuing her?

All was quiet except for a distant cathedral bell that rang nine times, which meant it was 9:00 p.m. She wondered why this office building was open so late in the evening. She thought of the cell phone she'd taken from the boys then thrown back to them. She regretted this now. They hadn't been able to catch it, and it was probably useless once it hit the pavement. Meanwhile, she was in bad need of a way to call the American Embassy. Then she remembered. Tomorrow was Saturday. The embassy would be closed. Even so, they must have a twenty-four seven emergency line. That brought up a new concern. She had to check out how much help the embassy would be willing to provide. According to Sergey Tarasov, the deputy minister who'd questioned her, the embassy didn't help U.S. citizens in trouble with Russian law enforcement. She wondered if this was true. She'd have to check it out before she contacted the embassy. But how was she going to do that without a computer or smartphone? Another worry popped into her head: If she couldn't get immediate help, where was she to stay? No hotel would accept her without a passport.

Nicole opened a door that led to the building's lobby. It was well lit, and there were windows through which she might be seen from outside. She decided to seek refuge on a higher floor. This thought lifted her spirits. Entering this building might turn out to be a lucky accident if she found an office she could get into. Maybe there would be a couch where she could bed down for the night.

She walked over to the elevators just as one of them dinged. She had the presence of mind to turn away as the doors slowly opened. As the passenger walked by, she risked a quick glance.

He was a middle-aged man whose downcast face and hunched shoulders made him look as if he was in a rush to escape a very bad day. He had no interest in her but was focused on getting out of the building as fast as he could.

The fact that someone was still here using the elevators made her decide to take the stairs. She spotted an arrow-shaped sign with the familiar staircase symbol and headed in that direction.

She climbed several flights until she came to a door marked with the number three. As soon as she stepped into the hallway, she saw that many of the offices were lit and appeared to be open for business. As she walked along, she noticed signs on the doors bearing the names of publications from all over the world: *Le Monde, The Guardian, China Daily, The Wall Street Journal, the Sydney Morning Herald,* and many others.

The offices were occupied by people busy at their computers. None of them looked up as she passed. This was the centralized media building that had been pointed out by the guide on the ship's tour of the city. It made sense that a country like Russia would want them all in one place. The government could keep track of phone calls and stories sent electronically. For that matter, they could bug the offices and listen in on conversations. She had no doubt this was done and that the reporters who worked here would be well aware of it.

In a building filled with journalists from all over the world—including the U.S. and U.K.—it was possible she could reach out and ask for help. But she was too frightened and exhausted from her last encounter with the police. She decided to wait until she calmed down. Maybe she could find an empty office and rest for a bit. Then she'd be better able to assess the situation and choose the most likely prospect.

She spotted a women's room and went in. When she looked in the mirror, she was shocked. Her coat was even dirtier and more worn than it had appeared in the hotel's uniform room. Her hair was a mess from running, and she had a dark smudge on one cheek.

She took off the coat and, draping it over her arm, washed her face, finger-combed her hair, and applied some lip gloss. These small touches made her slightly more presentable.

Further along the corridor, she noticed an office with the lights off and the door shut. The sign on the door identified it as *The Miami Herald*. It appeared to be closed for the night, perhaps the whole weekend. She reached into her purse for her Swiss Army knife in case she had to jimmy the lock. To her surprise, it was unlocked. She went in, closing and locking the door behind her.

The front office held two desks, each with a computer and stacks of newspapers. The floor was littered with crumpled computer printouts that had been tossed at the wastepaper basket and missed. There was a comfortable-looking couch, but she decided it would be a bad idea to sleep so close to a door where people entered. No telling how early they might arrive for work. She wanted to be able to hear them come in so she could hide and, hopefully, slip away before she was seen.

She headed through a doorway into a second office. This one looked as if it might belong to a bureau chief. It was larger than the outer office, although no neater. Since there was only one computer and one phone, whoever worked here must have the room to his or herself. It was furnished with a large desk piled with papers, two chairs facing the desk, a wall-mounted TV, and a daybed. A pillow and blanket were piled at one end as if someone slept or napped there. Nicole put her purse down and dropped onto the bed, kicking off her shoes. Getting off her feet and lying down felt unbelievably good. Only now did she realize how exhausted she was.

Her plan was to rest for a bit before seeing if she could sign onto one of the computers without a password. She wanted to find out if the news had anything that mentioned herself and Kat, or Darina Kravchenko, as well as check out the policies of the American Embassy. After that, she'd look around for someone she could ask for help.

Instead of a cat nap, she fell deeply asleep and didn't wake until dawn was beginning to light the sky. She hurried over to the desk and hit the enter key to wake up the computer. The browser was open and ready for business. Whoever had used the computer last had neglected to sign out. Maybe nobody bothered with a password here. What good would it do if the Russian government could hack into every computer and cell in the building?

She looked up Darina Kravchenko on the search engine and was shocked to see her own photo next to Kat's at the top of Pravda's website. She set the translation to English. The article was brief:

> The Moscow Police Department is currently looking for Nicole Graves, (above left) an American citizen who, along with Darina Kravchenko (above right), a Ukrainian national, murdered Sgt. Vladimir Ivanof, a 15-year veteran of the Moscow Police Force.
>
> Darina Kravchenko is now awaiting trial for Ivanof's murder and for the killing of Derek Swan, an American who drowned after being pushed from a cruise ship anchored in Moscow. It is not known if Ms. Graves was involved in Swan's death.
>
> Anyone who has seen Nicole Graves in the last 24 hours or who knows her whereabouts should contact the Moscow Police immediately. Police have warned the public not to approach Ms. Graves. She is considered armed and dangerous.

It was even worse than Nicole had feared. They'd made up the fictitious murder of a policeman and were trying to frame her and Kat for it. She wondered what their motive might be. Would they really cook up a murder charge because they thought she knew something about Derek Swan's death? Of course, she had escaped their custody, but she hadn't actually been arrested, which made this complete overkill. Kolkov was probably behind it. He must be taking some heat for letting her get away.

Next, she looked up the website of the American Embassy to see what help they offered Americans detained or arrested in Russia. She was shocked by how little they could do. Mainly, they offered services so unhelpful they were almost laughable. They would provide a list of English-speaking attorneys, contact family and friends with news of the arrest, and visit the prisoner to provide vitamins and reading materials. Even more striking was what they wouldn't or couldn't do, such as get U.S. citizens out of jail overseas, provide legal advice or represent U.S. citizens in court overseas, or pay their legal, medical, or any other fees.

Tarasov had been right. The American Embassy, which had been her best hope for escaping the police, would be no help at all. For all she knew, they might turn her over to the police if she showed up on their doorstep. With the smartwatch broken, getting in touch with her handler was an impossibility. The security agency—MI6 or whoever it was—hadn't received her message about the explosives hidden in Red Square. Presumably, they were still armed and ready to go off unless someone intervened. Now, with only two days left, the job of putting out a warning had fallen to her. But how? And to whom?

The sound of footsteps in the hallway sent her scurrying from the computer to a corner where she couldn't be seen through the window in the door. Her heart stopped racing when whoever it was passed the office and kept walking. The interruption made her wonder, once again, if someone who worked here might come in on a Saturday. She decided it would be a good idea to leave and check back later. She gathered up her things and turned out the lights. She left the door unlocked, just as she'd found it.

Nicole went to the women's room and once again tried to

make herself presentable. In her sleep-wrinkled clothes, this proved almost impossible. She gave up and left in search of some coffee. In the floor's opposite corner, she found a break room with vending machines. Attached to the wall was a change machine where she fed in some ruble notes and got back coins. After the frustration of her morning, this very normal activity somewhat calmed the turmoil raging inside of her.

Predictably, the vending machine contained mostly candy and chips, but the last choice on the bottom row was Cadbury chocolate chip brunch bars, a special favorite of hers. She'd only been able to get them in England and wondered how they'd ended up here in Moscow. She bought three and ate two while standing by the machine, putting the third one in her purse for later. She sipped the coffee while heading back to the *Miami Herald's* office. She was hoping it was still empty. With a little luck, she'd be able to use it as a hideout for the weekend while she figured out what to do next.

As she rounded the corner, she could see the office door was open and the light was on. She walked by slowly so she could look inside. A woman was at work on one of the computers. She was young, probably in her early twenties, with short dark hair. Dressed casually in jeans and a beige, long-sleeved T-shirt, she was frowning at her computer as if it were a puzzle she was trying to work out.

Nicole walked on, debating what to do. She was completely without resources. At some point, she'd have to take a leap and trust someone who might be able to help. This woman appeared to be a journalist. What better way to get her help than by offering her an exclusive story? It would be especially tempting to someone young, just starting out and trying to make a name for herself. Nicole turned and headed back to the office.

The woman didn't seem to notice when Nicole entered. "Sorry to interrupt," Nicole said. "Can I talk to you a minute?"

The woman turned to look at her, obviously startled. She stared at Nicole a moment before she stood up, eyes wide in surprise.

"Oh, my God!" she half whispered. "You're the woman whose photo was in Pravda."

Nicole was about to offer a defense, but the woman put her finger to her lips and waved her into the back office. She closed the door and turned the TV on with the volume up. Then she said, "The place is bugged. Tell me why the police are after you, but keep your voice low."

"They say I'm wanted for murder, but it's a lie," Nicole whispered. "I didn't kill anyone, and I doubt there's even a murdered policeman. The real story is that they think I witnessed a murder and tried to detain me as a witness by taking my passport and locking me in a hotel room. But I escaped. They made up the murder charge hoping it will motivate someone to turn me in. I'm not armed or dangerous, just a tourist who happened to be in the wrong place at the wrong time. Listen, what happened to me could be a front-page story under your byline in the *Miami Herald*."

The woman only took a moment before she smiled and held out her hand to shake Nicole's. "I'm Abby Hewitt," she said, her accent clearly American. "I'm not with the *Miami Herald*, but I'd love an exclusive interview. The *Herald* closed this bureau a few years ago. They rent office space to freelancers like me trying to make a name here so I can land a job back in the States. Right now, I'm barely making it as a stringer for a few small papers back home. Not the *Miami Herald*, though. They've made cutbacks and no longer use freelancers."

Once they were seated, Abby said, "When you say the police lied, I believe you. A friend of mine was arrested a few months ago covering a protest march. They hit him with a fake charge of assaulting a policeman. He's still locked up, awaiting trial. Believe me, I know what the police here are like."

Nicole gave Abby a bare outline of her story, leaving out any reference to her work for intelligence or the bomb in Red Square. Then she added, "I need a place to hide for a few days. If you can help, I'll give you an exclusive interview. It's a cautionary tale of how an innocent tourist can be swept up in Russia's criminal justice system. I'm sure you know their prosecutors' conviction rate. They can arrest and try me for murder, and it won't matter that there was never a body."

"I know," Abby said. "And you're right. It will make a great story. Are you sure there's no chance of getting back your passport?"

"Maybe, if you know a forger who'll do it on the cheap."

"What about the American Embassy? In a case like this, I'd think they'd issue you emergency travel papers and spirit you out of the country."

"Not with Russia claiming I'm a murderer." Nicole explained what she'd learned about the embassy's policy.

Abby frowned. "That's hard to believe. Are you sure?" Without waiting for an answer, she went to the computer and typed in something, then went quiet as she read what came up. "Oh, my God, you're right. They'll bring you vitamins? Seriously?"

"Hm. What are we going to do with you? I have an idea, but I have to make a call first to make sure my friend is willing." Abby disappeared into the front office and was back in a few minutes. Whoever she'd spoken hadn't needed much persuasion.

"I've got a place for you," Abby said. "But we have to take Metro to get there. Before you go out in public, you'll need a makeover so you won't be recognized. Let's start by getting you out of those wrinkled clothes. It looks like you've been sleeping in them."

Abby took the coat draped over Nicole's arm and held it up to get a look at it. "Ew, that's disgusting. Throw it away." She gestured toward a large waste bin by the desk. While Nicole took off her wrinkled turtleneck and slacks—which had been fresh from the cleaners when she put them on the day before—and Abby opened a closet, rifling through an assortment of garments hanging inside.

"A lot of freelancers who passed through this office left stuff," Abby said. "Some of it might belong to people who currently work here, but let's not worry about that." She gathered up several items and brought them over to the desk. "Do you have any makeup with you?"

The two of them went to work sitting side by side at the big desk. Nicole put out the makeup she carried in her purse, along with a small mirror. Abby supplemented this with eye shadow, eye liner, and contouring powder, which did its magic to change the shape of Nicole's face. The clothes Abby had left on the desk turned out to be a print dress, a midnight blue coat with an imitation fur collar, a hairband with fake black bangs, and a blue-and-white scarf. The dress was big and baggy, but the coat, which had a nipped-in waist and flared skirt, fit perfectly.

Abby put the hairband with the attached black bangs on Nicole. It was all wrong with Nicole's blond hair, but as soon as Abby tied the scarf kerchief-style around Nicole's head, the bangs became fairly convincing.

When she was fully outfitted, she studied herself in the full-length mirror on the back of the closet door. She looked different all right. The only problem was that the coat, with its tight-fitting waist and full, flared skirt, appeared to be part of an ice-skating costume. This, along with the kerchief, made her look as if she'd just stepped out of an earlier era, perhaps the 1930s.

Nicole took off the scarf and poked through the closet for something more contemporary. She found a dark green baseball cap with a Cyrillic word embroidered on the front. When Abby got a look at it, she gave a snort of laughter.

"What does it say?" Nicole said.

"It says 'Shut up.'"

"Will that cause problems?"

"Not really. It is a bit jarring with your sweet little face, but it's fine, really. Nobody pays attention to mottos on clothes here anyway. You mentioned that you just needed to hide for a few days," Abby said. "What happens then?"

"Hopefully, I'll be able to reach a friend who has influence in certain circles. He knows people who can arrange to get me out of the country." She paused, considering how much of the truth she should reveal. "But he was in an accident. He was taken to a hospital, and I don't know how to find him. Maybe you can help."

"Sure. What can I do?"

"Could you call around to hospitals and see if a man was admitted night before last with a gunshot wound?"

"Gunshot wound?" Abby said. "Wow. This story is getting more interesting by the minute."

"What about this?" Nicole said. "Say you're doing a story about gun violence in the city. Ask how many gunshot victims were admitted in the last few days. If there's a lot, narrow it down to night before last. If you could find my friend, I'd be able to visit him, and he'll let me know how to reach someone who can help."

"I don't know if the hospitals will give out information like that, but I'll try," Abby said. "What's your friend's name?"

"Chet—" Nicole paused, trying to summon up his last name. She'd only heard it once, when he introduced himself. "Antonovich. That's it. I'm so stressed out I can hardly remember my own name."

"I don't blame you," Abby said. "I'm dying to hear what happened to you. Can't you tell me more?"

"Not now. I will give you an exclusive interview, but not until I'm safely out of the country. You understand, don't you?"

"I do. Right now I'm bringing you to a friend who's willing to take you in," Abby said. "She said she's going out around noon. We'd better leave now."

CHAPTER NINE

THE MEDIA BUILDING WAS SEVERAL BLOCKS from a Metro station. As they walked, Abby described the woman who'd agreed to hide Nicole for a few days.

"At first, Olga will seem sort of—to put it bluntly— a little nuts," Abby said. "But that's an act she puts on in case anyone's watching. When I mentioned you, she already knew about your problems with the police. She'd seen the story about an American tourist being wanted for murder and immediately went online to find out more about you. She definitely wants to help. I expect she'll be waiting for us in front of her building. Don't let it throw you when she starts talking to you in Russian. Just call her "*babushka*" and act thrilled to see her, like you're her long-lost granddaughter or something. Whatever she does, just go with it. She'll explain once you're inside."

By now, they were descending a very long escalator into the Metro system. This station appeared to have been built in the era when the beauty of the subway was a major priority for the USSR. Nicole had seen another station from this period on the ship's city tour. This one featured polished marble walls, art-deco chandeliers, and bronze bas relief artwork. The ceilings were arched as were the openings to passageways leading from the main corridor to the subway lines.

Abby took in Nicole's awed expression as she gazed around.

"Yeah," Abby said. "It's really something, isn't it?" Once they boarded a train, the two limited themselves to small talk, chatting about home: L.A. for Nicole and Fort Lauderdale for Abby.

Abby made a wide gesture that took in her surroundings. "I was determined to get away from my home town, and, boy, did I."

"Do you plan to stay in Russia?"

"No way. I'm going home as soon as I land a job at a news outlet. I'd prefer print, but I can't afford to be fussy with so few jobs available. It seems I've picked the wrong century to go into journalism.

"What about you?" Abby said. "What do you do when you're not running from the police?" When Nicole explained what she did, Abby was astonished. "A private detective? I didn't even know they still existed. Do you, like, break into hotel rooms and take pictures of husbands cheating on their wives?"

Nicole laughed. "Private detectives used to do that, it's true. Maybe some still work on marital infidelity, but most states have no-fault divorce now, so those cases have pretty much gone away." She went on to explain that Colbert & Smith mainly handled cases for large corporations and law firms.

"What were you working on that made the police go after you?"

"I wasn't. I was on vacation. I'm just another American tourist."

Abby didn't comment, leaving Nicole to wonder if the young woman bought her story. They remained silent while the train passed through three more stations, each decorated in a unique way. Abby stood up as the train approached the next stop. "This is us." She led Nicole past several blocks of old, run-down apartment houses. At last she stopped and waved at an old woman seated on the stoop of a building up ahead. The woman looked bulky in her heavy coat, which she wore with a number of scarves, including one she'd fashioned into a turban.

"That's Olga," Abby said. "Remember, 'babushka' is the only

word you need to say. And whatever she does—hugs, kisses, and all—just go with it."

At the sight of Nicole, Olga stood up and cried out, "*Malyshka!*" followed by a string of other exclamations that sounded like terms of endearment. She hobbled down the stairs and pulled Nicole into a bear hug. Nicole responded, putting her arms around the old woman and calling out, "Babushka!" in what she hoped was a joyous voice. This was difficult when Olga was squeezing her so tightly. Nicole had expected Abby to stop for a visit, but without greeting Olga or saying goodbye to Nicole, she turned and headed back toward the Metro.

When Olga's welcome wound down, she put an arm around Nicole and guided her up the steps. The entry hall was as run-down as the building's exterior. It had a worn wooden floor, and the stairs they started to climb were covered with ancient, fraying carpet. They kept going until they reached the fourth or fifth floor; Nicole had lost track. Here, Olga took a jangling set of keys out of her pocket. After unlocking several deadbolts, she led Nicole inside. She signaled for Nicole to remain silent while Olga herself kept up a running monologue in Russian.

The place was the smallest studio apartment Nicole had ever seen, no more than eighty square feet, with worn but colorful, patterned rugs on the floor and hanging on the walls. The bed, covered with a lumpy duvet, took up most of the room. A tiny stove, sink, and refrigerator—all equally ancient—occupied one corner.

Olga opened a closet and gestured for Nicole to follow her inside. The old woman closed the closet door, plunging them into darkness while she felt around for a light switch and turned it on. She pulled aside a section of the wall and bent down to pass through the opening into a room no bigger than the one they'd just left. In contrast, it was neat and uncluttered. It held a couple of filing cabinets, several bookcases, and a desk with a computer and phone on top. An overstuffed chair and reading lamp sat in front of the desk. The furnishings looked fairly new. Against the wall was a futon with a pillow and blankets folded neatly on top.

Olga took off her scarves and coat and unwrapped the turban, hanging them on a coat rack near the door. The person who'd been hidden underneath all these clothes was much different than Nicole had pictured. For one thing, she didn't look like a loving babushka. She was the right age, perhaps in her seventies, but with a dancer's body, slender and upright. She must have been a great beauty, and she still remained attractive despite the passage of time. She had a cloud of silver curls, an angular face, and high cheekbones, but there was something hard and indomitable about her, and Nicole felt uncomfortable under her gaze. It was as if those piercing blue eyes could read her mind and see into her soul.

"Have a seat." Olga's English was clearly American. Nicole sat on the chair, while Olga settled across from her at the desk. "I understand you need a place to hide out from the police. I read Pravda's version. What really happened?"

Nicole explained about witnessing the murder, Kolkov's suspicion that she was hiding something, and his demand that she give evidence against her shipboard companion. She described the events that led up to meeting Abby. She finished with a greatly abbreviated version of Chet's shooting, adding that Abby was trying to locate him.

"Ah-hah," Olga said. "I hope that outfit you're wearing is a good disguise. The police will be scouring the city for you."

"It is. I don't look anything like Nicole Graves, believe me."

Olga looked at her watch. "It's coming up on noon. I'll fix us lunch. You can come with me, but we can't speak English in the other room. The walls in this building are like paper except for my den here, which I reinforced with acoustical tiles. I never speak English in there. The neighbors think I'm crazy." She smiled. "I put a lot of work into sustaining that image. They have no idea of my true identity, and I want to keep it that way."

Nicole accompanied Olga back to the other room, where the woman made egg salad sandwiches and hot tea in tall glasses with metal holders. They brought their food into Olga's den and resumed their seats, using the desk as a table.

"Do you mind if I ask how you ended up here?" Nicole said. "I can tell from your accent that you're American, and I'm guessing you grew up in New York."

"Clever girl! I went to Harvard, believe it or not. I'd skipped a couple of grades in high school, so I was sixteen when I entered the university, young and naive and impressionable. One of my professors was a devout communist. He became my mentor, then my lover, and I joined the communist party. This was in the 1960s. You can't imagine how difficult life was for communists in the U.S. back then. We were considered the enemy. I couldn't get a job. My family disowned me. I was thrown from a comfortable life into poverty and shunned by people I'd once considered friends.

"I decided I didn't belong at Harvard, in Boston, or the U.S., for that matter. I quit school and defected to Soviet Russia. I never saw my family again. It took about ten years for me to become disillusioned with my new country. By now, it was the late 1970s, and I'd started working with dissidents who were helping Jews escape from Russia. At the time, they weren't permitted to leave, but the group was heavily infiltrated with KGB. I was arrested, convicted of crimes against the state, and locked up for three years. I came out more determined than ever to remain in Russia and help others who were being persecuted." She stood up. "Excuse me, I'm going to get more tea. You probably want a refill, too. I'll bring the pot."

When Olga returned, she was carrying a tray with the teapot and a plate of small, round cookies covered with powdered sugar.

"Snowballs!" Nicole said. "I haven't had these in years. My mother used to make them, too."

Olga drew herself up in mock affront. "Snowballs? I'll have you know, my dear, that these are Russian tea cakes. And I don't bake. I buy them at the corner bakery."

Helping herself to a cookie, Nicole said, "It sounds like you've had a hard life."

"At times. But I believe that everything we experience, both good and bad, leaves us that much wiser. Things are good for me now, although I'd rather not have to pretend to be crazy. I help journalist friends like Abby find stories that tell the rest of the world what it's like in today's Russia. Sometimes I can help people like you, who are persecuted by the police. I have friends who are sympathizers and provide enough financial support to keep me and my cause afloat. I've never fit in anywhere, but now I do, in my own particular way. I'm doing something worthwhile by fighting the government and helping give voice to the opposition."

The phone on Olga's desk rang. Nicole noticed the ringer had been turned down so it was barely audible. Olga carried on her end of the conversation in Russian. When she hung up, she said, "That was Abby. She's getting pretty fluent in Russian. She wants you to know that she's still trying to find your friend. It isn't easy to get information out of hospitals. But she called someone at the ministry of health who owes her a favor, and he gave her a way to look in hospital records for recent gunshot victims. There are close to one hundred hospitals in Moscow, so it's taking a while. She did find two unidentified victims." Olga held up a sheet of paper where she'd written the hospitals' names. "The hospitals want to notify any family these people might have. And, of course, the police want to know more about them, why they were shot, and by whom. The men were found in different parts of the city, so there's no reason to think the shootings were related."

"Can you give me directions for getting there? I need to find

Chet as soon as possible."

"Of course," Olga said. "But first, I have to make you an ID card. All Russians and non-Russian residents have to carry them. You'll probably be asked for it when you visit the hospitals. First, I'll need a photo of you, of course." She went over to the filing cabinet and took out an old polaroid camera. She held it up, got it in focus, and said, "Look at the camera."

Nicole smiled as the camera clicked.

Olga shook her head. "We can't use that because you were smiling. This isn't the U.S., remember? Try to keep a serious face." Nicole obliged, and this time, Olga seemed satisfied and put the camera on her desk while the film rolled out and started to develop.

"Now I'll get to work on your ID. Tell me your friend's last name. I'll use it on the card so it looks like you're married. Most hospitals won't let you visit a patient unless you're a close relative."

"It's Antonovich."

"Antonovich," Olga repeated, writing it on a notepad. "Making up an ID takes a little while. There's a stack of newspapers on the filing cabinet. You might want to read while I take care of this."

Nicole looked through the papers. Only two were in English, *The Guardian* and the *New York Times International Edition*, but the most recent was a week old. Nicole tried to focus on the *New York Times*, but she was too keyed up and anxious. She decided to explore Olga's bookshelves instead. She was curious about the woman, and her choice of books might reveal more about her.

"Do you mind if I look through your books?"

"Not at all. Help yourself."

About half the books were in Russian, the rest in English. Olga's taste appeared very similar to Nicole's; they both had an appreciation for literary fiction. She spotted a copy of Margaret Atwood's *The Handmaid's Tale*, one of her favorites. Next to it was *The Testaments*, the Handmaid's sequel, which Nicole had been meaning to read. She pulled it down from the shelf and an envelope fell out. Handwritten in large, flowing script on the envelope was the name "Olga Whitney Marozova." There was no address or postage stamp, so it must have been hand-delivered.

Nicole glanced over at Olga to be sure she wasn't looking and, turning way, slipped the letter out of the envelope. It said:

"My greatest hope was that we could be together and share what little time we have left. You've made it clear you aren't interested. I accept your decision and will stop calling since I now realize my persistence has upset you. I've left this parting gift. Love always, Max."

She opened the book and read the inscription on the title page, written in the same hand. "To Olga, with love and admiration. You will never let something like this happen to us." It was signed, "Max."

She carefully tucked the note back in the envelope, which she slipped into the book before sitting down and starting to read. She was only a few pages in when Olga handed her the finished ID card. It was still warm from the thermal laminator. It looked authentic, although Nicole was in no position to judge. Her photo was on it, along with print beneath it in Cyrillic.

"I've made you a legal resident from Slovakia," Olga said. "You came here when you married Antonovich. This would explain why you don't speak Russian, and most Russians don't speak Slovak. Your name is Nicola Pavlikova Antonovich. Now, let's see. What else do you need?"

"Directions for getting to the hospitals," Nicole said.

Olga picked up the notes she'd made earlier and handed them over. Then she pulled a small pamphlet out of her desk. "Here are some Russian phrases that might come in handy. They include English definitions as well as transliteration, so you shouldn't have too much trouble pronouncing them. Since you're Slovakian, they'll understand why you aren't fluent in Russian.

The one phrase you should memorize is 'I am his wife.'"

Olga opened a desk drawer, took out a burner phone still in its wrapper, and handed it to Nicole. "You shouldn't go anywhere without a way to communicate. Let me have those papers again. I want to write down my phone number in case you run into any problems."

"Can I use this phone to call home for my phone messages? I haven't picked them up in a while, and that worries me."

Olga went into her desk again and pulled out a different phone. "Here, this one has enough credit on it for you to call overseas. Make it short, or it will run out of its allotment."

"Thanks," Nicole said, exchanging the original phone for the new one. She was putting on her coat when Olga said, "Wait! I forgot one last thing. She went over to the filing cabinet, opened the top drawer, and reached into it, pulling out a small box. Inside was a plain gold band, a wedding ring, that was dulled from years of wear. She slipped it onto the ring finger of Nicole's right hand. "Now you're properly married to this Antonovich. I hope he's tall, dark, and handsome."

"More like very, very tall and fair. Not exactly handsome, but sort of hot."

"Is he your lover?"

"No. I'm engaged, and my fiancé really is tall, dark, and handsome."

"So? Where is this Mr. Tall, Dark, and Handsome who leaves you to take a cruise on your own?"

"It's complicated," Nicole said.

Olga smiled. "I'll bet it isn't as complicated as he wants you to think. Why don't you give this friend of yours a try? What were the words to that song? 'If you can't be with the one you love, love the one you're with.'"

"I'm afraid that isn't in my nature. I'm hopelessly monogamous."

The two bid each other goodbye and Nicole left, heading for

the Metro. The ride took about forty minutes, time enough for Nicole to go over the sheet of Russian phrases and practice them silently in her head. The hospital was part of a large medical complex spread over several blocks of almost identical buildings, gray with darker gray double columns between each row of windows. It looked relatively new, and the grounds were neatly landscaped.

The woman at the front desk asked for Nicole's ID and took a quick look at the photo before handing it back. Nicole consulted the list of phrases Olga had given her and asked to see her husband. She only referred to him by his last name. She was pretty sure he didn't go by "Chet" in this country.

The woman looked through names on her computer and said, "*Nyet.*" She gestured to the man waiting behind Nicole to step up to the counter.

Instead of making way for him, Nicole looked at her list of phrases and read the word *unconscious*. She must have mispronounced it because the woman didn't understand. Nicole stuck out her finger as if her hand were a gun and pointed to her side and mimed someone asleep or unconscious.

For the first time, the woman looked directly at her, her eyes reflecting understanding and perhaps sympathy. She quickly scrolled through the records again as if she knew what she was looking for. When she stopped scrolling, she said "Ah!" then started explaining something to Nicole in Russian. Nicole gestured with a shrug, signaling that she didn't understand. The woman jotted the number 437 on a slip of paper, gave it to Nicole, and pointed to the elevators on the other side of the lobby.

It took Nicole a while to find the room. The place was enormous, and she kept having to ask for directions, pointing to the paper with the room number and making it clear she didn't speak Russian. Several times she had to backtrack where someone had steered her wrong or, more probably, she'd misunderstood the directions. Finally she found room 437. There were four patients crowded into a room barely adequate for two. They were walled off from each other by screens that appeared to be made of cardboard. The room was overheated and smelled heavily of cigarette smoke. As she gazed around, she could see that the smoke was concentrated around a bed in one corner. She slowly walked past the beds, observing the occupants. One man was too old, the second too young, and the third too small. None of them had their eyes open, and it was hard to tell if they were asleep or unconscious. But Chet wasn't among them. She peeked into the corner where the smoker was lying. This man was wide awake, bald, with a fringe of dark hair. He winked at Nicole and blew a couple of smoke rings, then gave her an enormous smile from which two teeth were missing.

Out of pity, Nicole smiled back and waved before hurrying down to the lobby. As she emerged from the elevator, the woman at the counter motioned her over and said something in Russian. This time, Nicole didn't need to understand the words. The woman wanted to know if she'd found her husband. Nicole gave a sad shake of her head.

As she walked toward the exit, she looked at the clock. It was 4:00 p.m. She didn't know how long it would take to get to the next hospital, but it didn't matter. Time was running out, and she had to follow every lead. She had only two more days until the Victory Day celebration. If she couldn't find someone to help, she'd decided, the British Embassy would be a better bet than her own. They might know who to contact. How much would she have to tell them? Everything, she supposed, and she hoped the people who worked there would believe her and could be trusted. She had no idea if this was the right thing to do, but she had no other choice.

The second hospital was just as enormous as the first. The architecture was similar except that the front of this building was crescent shaped with a driveway that circled up to the front entrance and rounded back out to the street. The lobby setup was almost identical, too, with one person behind the counter to handle visitors' questions.

From a distance, the receptionist looked like the prototypical jolly babushka who'd be greatly loved by all who knew her. But as Nicole got closer, she could see the woman wore a sour expression. She looked as if she were fed up with the day, the people she had to talk to, and perhaps the whole world. Without looking at Nicole, the woman silently pointed to her left, where at least thirty people were queued up to be helped. Nicole went to the end of the line and waited quite a while before she reached the counter.

The receptionist requested Nicole's ID and held on to it. When Nicole asked for a patient named Antonovich, the woman couldn't find him in the directory, and she was much less patient than the receptionist at the other hospital. When Nicole indicated she didn't speak Russian, the woman turned on a loudspeaker and made an announcement. Nicole wondered if she was calling security and toyed with the idea of making a quick exit.

Before she could do so, a friendly looking young man in a suit and tie walked up to her. He turned out to be an interpreter. The desk clerk had summoned him because of Nicole's inability to understand Russian. She handed Nicole's ID to him. Nicole's stomach lurched. If by chance he knew Slovak, he'd know she wasn't Slovakian because she couldn't speak the language any more than she could speak Russian. He'd figure out her ID must be forged and turn her over to the police.

But luck was with her. The interpreter didn't speak Slovak, and to her relief, their only common language was the French she'd studied in school. She could catch the gist of what he said, but her ability to speak French had all but disappeared. She managed to make herself understood mainly by gesturing when she couldn't remember a word. She explained about the bullet wound and that she and her husband had been mugged, his wallet and ID stolen. If he was unconscious, the hospital wouldn't have his name in their records, but he might still be here.

Much to the annoyance of the desk clerk, the interpreter interrupted her while she was helping another visitor. When the interpreter explained Nicole's dilemma, the woman went into her computer, looked up a record, and printed it out. She handed it to the interpreter and spoke to him in a low voice.

He came back to where Nicole was waiting. He explained that a patient with a gunshot wound was brought in night before last, but he'd died. His body was still there, waiting for the coroner to pick him up. "It would be good if you could identify him," he said. "Do you feel you able to do that?"

Nicole nodded yes, and the man accompanied her to the elevator where he hit the button for the bottom floor. She'd had to identify a corpse once before in a case back home. It hadn't been too unpleasant since they'd showed her a photo of the dead girl, and she didn't have to look at the body. Here, there were no such niceties. When the interpreter led her down to the basement morgue, the air was heavy with the unmistakable smell of human decay.

The interpreter spoke to the attendant, and the man went over to a bank of stainless-steel drawers and pulled one out. When the corpse's face was uncovered, it was clear that—aside from the bullet that killed him—the man had been badly beaten and someone had virtually pulverized his face. Even so, she could tell from his physique that it wasn't Chet. She was so relieved that she almost cried. She must have appeared on the verge of collapse because the interpreter grabbed her arm and steered her over to a chair.

She didn't sit for long. Her only desire was to leave this place and its terrible smell. On the Metro ride back to Olga's, she wondered if Chet might have died before they got him to the hospital. If he was never admitted as a patient, he probably would have been sent straight to the city morgue, and she'd never find out what happened.

By the time she got back to Olga's, it was 7:00 p.m. Olga had set out a platter of potato-cheese pierogi she'd bought at a neighborhood shop. Under other circumstances, the food might have been appealing, but as Nicole explained, after her visit to the hospital's morgue, she was unable to look at the food, much less eat it. She apologized.

"No need, my dear," Olga said. "You must be exhausted. I usually read in bed during the evening. You can take the futon in my office, and I have a nightgown you can wear. Shall we make up the futon now?"

"Thanks, but I can do that myself."

Olga gave her the bedding. They bid each other goodnight. Nicole ended up reading until the wee hours.

In the morning, she examined her face in the mirror of the tiny bathroom, expecting to see the bloodshot eyes and dark circles she'd earned from all the sleepless nights since this trip began. But she looked no different than usual. She still couldn't eat the toast and jam Olga had set out for breakfast, but she managed to down two cups of tea.

As they were getting up from the table, the phone rang. Olga picked it up, gave a brief response, and headed for the closet that led to her office. She beckoned Nicole to follow. Once they were in the office, she handed the phone to Nicole. "It's Abby," she said. "She wants to speak to you."

"I found him," Abby said. "I figured that if they couldn't ID him, they'd conclude he didn't have medical insurance so he'd end up at a free state hospital. But for some reason—probably because he'd lost a lot of blood and needed immediate care—they took him to a private hospital. They have his first name as Konstantin, by the way. "

"Really? I didn't think he had any ID on him."

"Maybe he told them."

"You mean he's conscious?"

"I got that impression. I told them I was his wife, so they're expecting a wife to visit him."

Nicole wrote down the name and address of the hospital and Abby's directions for getting there. As soon as she was dressed, Nicole headed out. This hospital was in a handsome new building with a bank of windows facing the park across the street.

She knew the routine now and what to say to the receptionist. She was given his room number and a sticker to wear on her lapel to show that she'd checked in. She felt hopeful and more upbeat than she had since Chet had said she'd be going home soon. If only that had been true.

She easily found the right wing of the hospital, but when she reached the corridor where his room was located, she stopped. A policeman was sitting on a chair in front of a patient's door. Nicole walked along the hallway, checking room numbers. As she'd suspected, the one guarded by the cop was Chet's. She couldn't go in, not while that policeman was sitting there. Was he protecting Chet because of the shooting or had Chet been arrested? She'd have to wait, hoping the cop would get up and leave so she could sneak in. She was pretty sure she could get the information she needed quickly, providing Chet was conscious.

She went into the women's room, peeking out every few minutes to see if the cop was still there. After a long wait, he got up and left. She didn't know how much time she had before he returned, but this was her chance. She hurried into the room.

Chet's eyes were closed, but as soon as she gave his shoulder a little shake, he opened them and gave her a blank look.

"Hi, Chet. It's Nicole, remember me?"

He stared at her for a long moment before he smiled. "Of course. I was supposed to pick you up, wasn't I? But I got shot. I don't remember anything after that. Was I on my way to you?"

Nicole took a deep breath and looked away. He had no recollection of the hours before he was shot, so he wouldn't remember where the explosives were. But it could have been worse. At least he was alive and awake; he knew who she was and remembered the purpose of their mission.

She dropped her voice to a whisper. "Your contact has to send someone to disarm the explosives in—"

"Yes, yes, now I remember. I was supposed to take you there so you could show me where they are."

"We went there, Chet," she said. "Don't you remember any of it?"

"Sorry. I can't—it must have something to do with my injury. Maybe it will come back to me."

"Listen, it's fine." As she spoke, Nicole took a pen and small notebook from her purse. "I'll take care of it. Just tell me how to get in touch with your handler."

He beckoned her closer and whispered, "I'll tell you, but you can't write it down, or it might get into the wrong hands. You'll have to commit it to memory. You understand?"

Just then, the door opened, and the policeman walked in. Seeing Nicole he shook his head and grabbed her arm muttering, "Nyet, nyet." He pulled her to her feet and began steering her toward the door.

She recalled the Russian phrase Olga had told her to memorize: "I am his wife."

The policeman let go of her and said something, pointing to his watch then holding up one hand and waggling all five fingers. She took this to mean he'd let her stay five minutes. As he left, he closed the door.

"Why is the policeman here?" Nicole said.

"He's waiting to see if my memory comes back. The police want to know why I was shot. Maybe they think it has something to do with the Russian Mafia. I keep telling them I don't remember, but it was probably a mugging since my wallet and ID are gone. He'll probably give up by the end of the afternoon. A mugging is of little consequence to the Moscow police."

"OK," she whispered. "All I need is that phone number. Then I can leave and let your contact know about the explosives and where to find you."

He motioned for her to sit on the bed and move close enough for him to whisper in her ear. He recited a phone number, and she repeated it back enough times until it was firmly planted in her memory.

She started to get up, but he said, "Wait!" She leaned down again for him to whisper in her ear.

"There's a passphrase I have to repeat to identify myself. It's 'I'm looking for a bargain price on a case of vodka.'"

"Got it!" She stood up again. "Thanks and goodbye. I hope you'll be back on your feet soon."

"No worries. I heal fast. I'll be out of here in a day or two."

She opened the door to find herself face-to-face with the policeman. He'd been on his way in to say her time was up. He asked her something in Russian. She shrugged as if to say she didn't know the answer to his question. Before he could pursue it, Chet called out to him. The policeman hesitated and watched Nicole walk away before he disappeared into Chet's room.

CHAPTER TEN

NICOLE DUCKED INTO A HOSPITAL BATHROOM and used the burner phone to call the number Chet had given her. The phone rang once before a recorded message came on. It was in English and terse: "This number is no longer in service." After the message, it immediately disconnected. She hung up and tried again in case she'd made a mistake the first time, but the result was the same.

She understood what this meant and felt a slow burn of anger. They'd shut down Chet's ability to communicate with them, and in so doing, they'd cut her off, too—completely pulled the rug out from under the two of them. She grew even more outraged when she thought of all she'd gone through for this assignment—the horror of witnessing a murder, the anxiety of dealing with the Russian police, the need to flee into a city where she knew no one. Ian Davies had completely misled her. According to him, she could expect a pleasant cruise on the Volga, spending a little time observing a handful of fellow passengers and filing some reports.

What Chet was going through was much worse. His handler must have found out he'd been shot and was in the hospital under police guard. Perhaps intelligence was afraid he might let it slip that he was a spy, and the Russians would find a way to extract more information from him. She wondered if the Brits had given up on the whole operation. Would they really back off, let Red

Square blow up, and allow the Ukraine to suffer Russia's terrible vengeance?

What now?

Today was May 8. The Victory Day parade was tomorrow, and British intelligence's attempt to prevent the destabilization of Eastern Europe seemed to have fallen apart.

Nicole decided to return to Olga's and try to figure out what, if anything, she could do. If she went to the British Embassy and told them what she knew, would they believe her? Or would they think she was some kind of conspiracy nut? She now realized they wouldn't know anything about Chet or his assignment for MI6. That would be beyond top secret. She felt compelled to do something to stop the impending disaster. She just couldn't imagine what that might be.

It was late morning when she arrived at Olga's building and climbed the many flights of stairs to her apartment. She knocked at the door, but there was no answer. Maybe Olga was in the office and hadn't heard. She tried again and again, knocking louder each time until she was convinced the woman wasn't home. She sat on the floor in front of the apartment for nearly an hour, wondering what might have happened to Olga. Was it possible she'd been caught and arrested? It had happened before. This new worry joined her concern for Chet and the explosives in Red Square.

Anxiety drove Nicole out of the building. She settled on the apartment's front stoop. Here, at least, she had the mild distraction of watching what was happening on the busy boulevard. Before long, who should come doddering along the sidewalk but Olga in her babushka outfit. She was dragging a dilapidated shopping cart filled with grocery bags. Nicole was overjoyed to see her. The old woman greeted her once more with a delighted "Malyshka!" and they hugged. Nicole took over bumping the shopping cart up the stairs while Olga hobbled beside her, letting out an occasional groan as if her knees were killing her.

Once inside the apartment, they headed for the office so they could talk. As Olga shed her coat and layers of scarves, Nicole told her about the disconnected phone. She was careful not to use the word "handler" or give any hint that Chet was a spy. Instead, she said that since she couldn't reach Chet's "friend," she had no way of getting out of the country.

"Have you picked up your own voice messages yet?" Olga said. When Nicole shook her head, Olga went on, "Why don't you take care of that? It will give you something to do, and one of those calls might be important. Be sure to use the burner, not my home phone." Olga pulled out a pen and pad of paper, put them on her desk, and got up to offer Nicole her seat. "I'm going back to the kitchen to put my groceries away."

Nicole called the international number for mobile customer support, which she'd jotted in her notebook. This time a real person answered after she negotiated the choices on the phone menu. At last, she was able to pick up her messages. There were thirty waiting for her. She deleted several recorded sales pitches and a call from her boss, Jerry, who sounded contrite. She wondered if he finally realized he'd acted like a jerk and wanted to apologize. She saved calls from three friends so she could return them when—and if—she got home. There was a call from someone who threatened to turn off her utilities if she didn't call an 800 number to take care of a past-due bill. Since she had such bills paid automatically from her bank account, she knew this was a scam and deleted it. Cold calls had come in from realtors and building contractors trying to drum up business.

With most of the calls out of the way, she got to one that— to her astonishment—was from Reinhardt. He sounded as if no time had passed, and he expected to pick up where they'd left off all those months ago.

"Hey, baby, where are you? Guess what! I'm finally coming to L.A. I called your office, but you didn't pick up. Hope you get this message. Give me a call. Love you."

He'd left another message twelve hours later. "I'm here in L.A. standing outside the door to your condo. It's midnight and you aren't here. Now I'm worried something's happened to you. Please call me."

She paused after the second message, surprised to feel her eyes filling with tears. She was so happy to hear from him, to know he was all right. At the same time, she was furious. How many times had she left messages on his phone saying how worried she was? On her birthday, five months before, she'd received a hand-written note from him, but she'd never received a single response to her calls.

Another voice message had been left the previous morning. "I talked to your sister, and she told me you're on a tour of Russia. I called the touring company. They said you'd left the ship two days ago, and they had no idea where you were. I looked online and was gobsmacked to see you've made headlines over there. Apparently, you're a person of interest in a couple of murders and escaped police custody. Mother of God, Nicole! What are you doing in Russia of all places? And—I hate to sound like your old boyfriend—Jonah? Jeb? Whatever his name was—but how do you manage to keep putting yourself in harm's way like this? I'm in a cab heading for LAX to catch the next flight to Moscow.

"You know my number. Give me a call and let me know if you're still there. If I don't answer, leave a message with an address where I can find you. I'm scheduled to land at Domodedovo Airport around 10:00 a.m. Remember, all of my messages are encrypted, so you don't have to worry about hackers."

Right after this message was one from her sister. "Where are you? Reinhardt told me you left the cruise and are wanted by the Russian police. For God's sake, Nicole, what's going on? Call me."

Instead of returning Steph's call, she hurried into the kitchen to get Olga. Back in the relative privacy of the office, Nicole explained who Reinhardt was while remaining as vague as possible about his work.

"He's been away on business for a while and out of touch because he was so busy. But he called and left messages several times since I've been away. He read that the Moscow police are looking for me, and he's worried. So he's on his way here. In fact, he may already have landed. Is it OK with you if I give him your address?"

Olga gave her a long, searching look. "I see. This is spy business. Your friend Chet is a spy, this fiancé of yours, and maybe you, too. May I ask who you work for?"

Nicole was dumbfounded. How did Olga deduce this from so little information? "Believe me, I'm not a spy. Chet and Reinhardt are both British, but I don't know—" Her voice trailed off. She could see Olga wasn't buying it.

"Nicole," Olga said. "You are a very bad liar, or is it that you're naïve? Of course they're spies."

"All right. This is all I know. When I met him, Reinhardt was a DCI with the London Police. A while back, he changed jobs. Since then, he's refused to talk about his work."

"MI6, then." Olga nodded her head in a way that said she understood the situation perfectly.

"Truthfully," Nicole said. "I've suspected that myself. Last time we were together, he told me he'd burned out on the stress, constant travel, and loneliness of his work. He said he was going to resign and find work in L.A. so we could be together. That was when he proposed. He said he had to return to his office, formally resign, and hand his work over to someone else. That was eight months ago, and he's pretty much ghosted me ever since."

"You see?" Olga said. "That's because he can't bring himself to give up the life. These people never can." She got up from the table and started pacing, her mouth set in a thin, angry line. "I've known men like him. In fact, I was married to one. Or thought I was. But he was already married to his work. When I gave him an ultimatum—me or the spy business—he chose spying."

Olga stopped pacing and settled at the table again, still agitated. "You asked if you could give this man my address, and I'm afraid the answer is no. I'm sorry, but how can you be sure these messages are really from your fiancé? It could be a trick. Have him meet you at a public place so you can see him before he sees you. There's a café called Shokoladnitsa about a block away. It has a big window, and it's easy to see who's inside from the street. Promise me you'll wait outside until you see him enter. Once you're sure it's him, he's welcome here. With the police looking for you, I wouldn't advise you to go to a hotel, but he can stay with you in my office."

Nicole nodded. "You're right. I was so happy to hear from him that I didn't think. But I'm certain that was him on the phone. I know his voice."

She returned to Olga's office to make the call. Reinhardt picked up right away. When she told him to meet her at the cafe, he said, "Isn't it risky to show your face in public with the police looking for you? Shouldn't I come to your place?"

"No. It will be fine. I have a good disguise. In fact, I dare you to recognize me! Don't be surprised if a strange woman drops by your table and tries to pick you up."

He laughed. "I'd know you anywhere."

"Don't count on it," Nicole said.

She gave him the location of the Shokoladnitsa café, and they agreed to meet at 2:00, which would give him time to get out of the airport and into the city. As soon as they hung up, Nicole returned her sister's call.

"For God's sake, Nicole," Steph said. "Come home. What phone are you using? It doesn't have caller ID."

"It's a burner phone. I lost my cell."

"Give me the number so I can get in touch with you. Where

are you staying? Are you safe? You aren't still wanted by the police, are you?"

"Everything's fine, but this is a borrowed phone, so you can't call me on it. Don't worry about me. I'm perfectly safe. I'll call you tomorrow." Nicole hung up before Stephanie could ask any more questions.

She returned to the kitchen. Since she wasn't meeting Reinhardt until 2:00 and it was only noon, she killed time helping Olga stuff envelopes with homemade pamphlets. They were written in Russian and turned out on a printer in bad need of a new ink cartridge.

"They aren't supposed to look professional," Olga explained when she noticed Nicole taking a close look at them. "They're for my neighbors here in the building."

"What do they say?" Nicole asked.

"Nothing important. I send these out every few weeks. They're part of my crazy act. This one complains about cockroaches in my apartment." Olga gave a little laugh. "As if everyone living in these old, government-built apartments doesn't have them. In my pamphlet I blame people in the building who leave food lying around. I insist that everyone contribute 1000 rubles to hire an exterminator. These people would never spend a kopek on their apartments, even if an exterminator could do anything about cockroaches. Next month I'll complain about something else, rats, strangers roaming the halls. Maybe I'll say I was mugged in the entry hall during broad daylight. Or I'll claim my apartment was burglarized, that it was someone in the building, and I know who it was." Olga laughed again. "Yes, I like that. This is the one part of my assumed identity I actually enjoy. It makes others in this building avoid me. They're afraid I'll harangue them with my complaints.

"Oh, I almost forgot." She handed Nicole a keyring with three keys on it. "In case you get locked out again. By the way, your makeup needs a touch-up. If there's anything you don't have, you'll find a cigar box full of cosmetics in the top drawer of my dressing table. And you can't possibly meet your fiancé wearing that horrid dress." As she spoke, she went to the closet that served as a passageway and brought back a couple of clothing bags. One of them held a classic beige sheath dress. The style dated back to the 1950s, but it was in mint condition. From the other bag, Olga pulled out a fur jacket of a slightly darker tone. The dress and jacket made a stunning outfit.

As Nicole thanked her, Olga was putting on her shapeless coat to distribute her flyers around the building. She draped scarves over her shoulders, leaving one to wrap around her head.

After Olga left, Nicole put on the dress. It was a bit long and slightly big but a distinct improvement over the one Abby had given her. Next she started working on her face at Olga's dressing table, which was equipped with a mirror. She took out the small supply of makeup she kept in her purse then located Olga's box, which contained a collection of surprisingly pricy cosmetics. They looked as if they'd been recently used. This made Nicole wonder if Olga sometimes went out made up as someone other than an eccentric old woman.

She spent the next half hour prettying up her disguise. She felt almost giddy at the prospect of seeing Reinhardt again. She dipped into Olga's cosmetics for a fresh stick of kohl to line her eyes, then added a pair of fake eyelashes she found in an unopened packet. When she was done, she slipped on the fur jacket. She'd just put on the hairband with the black bangs and the baseball cap, when Olga walked in.

"Ach! Don't spoil your looks with that hideous cap and fake hair," Olga chided. "You want to look beautiful. I have just the thing." She reached the closet and pulled out a black beret.

"But my hair! I can't go out with my blond hair showing."

Olga was silent as she tossed the fake bangs and baseball

cap onto her dressing table and put the beret on Nicole. She tucked Nicole's hair into it and angled it slightly toward one side. "Tres chic," she said, smiling at the effect. Nicole checked her appearance in the mirror. She did look rather glamorous. *Excellent*, she thought. She truly didn't recognize the woman in the mirror.

Nicole stood in a doorway across the street from the café and scanned the diners through the window. Reinhardt wasn't there. She fretted until she spotted him heading up the street from the direction of the Metro. He was wearing a tan trench coat and carrying an attaché case. He was walking briskly—he was in fact three minutes late—and had a smile of anticipation on his face. As soon as he was seated in the café, Nicole crossed the street and entered. He immediately spotted her and hurried over.

"Darling!" he said, pulling her into an embrace that lifted her momentarily off her feet—a restrained greeting in deference to Russian disapproval of public displays of affection. Then he put his arm around her and led her to a corner booth that offered some privacy from the other customers.

Reinhardt said, "See? I knew it was you right away. That is an excellent disguise, and you still manage to look beautiful. Well done."

She studied his face. She could tell by his expression that he was unrepentant for his long absence and failure to return her calls and messages.

"Tell me this," he said. "Why in the hell did you come to Moscow of all places? Both your sister and your boss said you hadn't mentioned vacation plans until a few days before—"

She'd expected some kind of apology, an explanation, but he didn't seem to realize he'd done anything wrong. Despite all the love she felt for him, she was suddenly filled with anger. "No. First I want you to explain," she said. "Why have you ghosted me all these months when you solemnly promised you'd join me in a

145

week? Where in the hell have *you* been?"

He opened his mouth as if to reply then closed it again. She could see her question had caught him by surprise. How could he be so clueless? All this time, he hadn't given her a thought.

By now she was steaming. "I'm waiting for an explanation," she said

"Well, you see—I, I mean—," he spluttered. "There was a case I'd spent months working on. When I went back to hand in my resignation, they told me my last effort had produced a breakthrough. Since I knew the case better than anyone, they wanted me to go back, put the pieces together, and supervise rounding up the suspects. These were terrorists conspiring to hit the U.K. with a cataclysmic attack. At first, we were only able to catch the lowest level operatives. We had the others on the run, but we were certain they hadn't given up their plan for a massive attack. It took time to round all of them up."

"You told me you were going to hand your cases over to someone else."

"But this was different. It was the biggest case of my career. Even so, you were on my mind the whole time. All I thought about was the day it would be over and I would be with you again."

"I still don't get it," she said. "Why didn't you pick up a phone or pen and paper and let me know?" She was almost shouting now, and she noticed people at other tables turning in their direction. She lowered her voice. "I'd have been disappointed and probably angry—but not as angry as I am right now. And at least I'd have known you were still alive and cared about me." Only when her eyes filled with tears did she realize how incensed she was and, at the same time, how heartbroken. He wasn't going to change. He was incapable of it. Olga was right.

She got up and headed for the door. Reinhardt got up to follow her, but the waiter was close on his heels demanding payment.

She could hear Reinhardt arguing with the waiter as she left the restaurant. He pointed out they hadn't ordered anything, but the waiter insisted they owed the minimum charge since they'd occupied a table during the midday rush. Nicole walked quickly in the direction of Olga's place. Only a few minutes passed before Reinhardt was beside her, breathing hard from running.

"I couldn't tell you," he said. "That's a strict policy when someone is on assignment. No communications home. I thought you knew that and would understand. And I did go against the rules to send you a note on your birthday."

She turned to face him, ready to continue berating him. But when she saw how stricken he looked, she burst into tears and let herself be folded into his arms.

"I'm sorry, I'm so sorry," he murmured into her hair.

She looked up at him. "What happens now? If the agency has an assignment of world-shattering importance, you'll drop everything and disappear again, won't you? You'll never be rid of them. This is a life sentence."

"No," he said. "I've officially resigned. We've severed all ties. They won't call me. I promise."

She looked at him. "The last time I saw you, you promised the same thing. You were resigning and that would be the end of it."

"And now I have officially resigned. I'm done. I know it may not sound different to you. But it is. I just didn't realize—" He put his hand under her chin and forced her to look at him. "I'm so terribly sorry to have hurt you. Will you give me another chance, or are you finished with me?"

She rested her head against his chest. "Forgiven, but not forgotten. This has to be the last time you disappear on me. I mean it. The very last."

He let out a sigh. "You have my word. Shall we go back to the restaurant and have lunch?"

She pulled a tissue out of her purse to wipe her eyes and blow her nose. "Not after I made a scene there. I'd rather go somewhere else."

They walked for a bit, silent but holding hands. When they came to a little café that looked clean, if not grand, they went in. After they were seated, they consulted the menu and ordered pickled herring and syrniki, which was described as cottage cheese pastries with sour cream and jam.

Once the waiter took their order, Reinhardt said, "Do you want to tell me why you're here, or am I forbidden to ask?"

"Now you're afraid of me," Nicole laughed. "I think I like it. But I do want to tell you what happened because I desperately need help." She went over the whole sequence of events since she'd met Ian Davies at the La Brea Tar Pits. When she was done, she added, "At first I thought it was you who'd suggested me for the assignment because I'd be good at observing these people. And I was hoping you'd be here. But there was no sign of you, and things started to go wrong. That's when I realized you'd never have put me in that position."

"You're right," he said. "It's too dangerous. In fact, I told them not to do it, but those bastards went ahead and recruited you anyway."

"You mean they asked your permission?"

"Not exactly. I'd managed to keep our relationship quiet until the human trafficking case in London last year. They looked into your background and discovered we'd been seeing each other off and on for a long time. They were impressed with your work and asked me if I thought you'd make a good operative. I said definitely not, that you were too emotionally fragile."

"Wait a minute!" Nicole felt her anger rising again.

"Sorry, I know that isn't true, but I didn't want you mixed up with them. When a case goes bad, they think a very long while before coming to an operative's aid, if they do it at all. Like that chap Antonovich in the hospital. Do you think the Brits are going to dispatch a Blackhawk to airlift him out of harm's way? They'll wait for him to figure his own way out, if he can. They'll never admit he's one of ours or that we have covert operatives in their country. But Chet appears to be an especially valuable operative. If all else fails, they'll probably work out a trade, giving Russia a couple of spies we're holding in an exchange. While the diplomats are working this out, he'll probably be locked up a good, long while. What makes me especially angry is that they brought you here without proper training or a realistic understanding of the risks. They're going to hear about this."

"Pardon me for asking, but why would they care what you think? You don't even work for them anymore. Right?"

"Why would they care?" He chuckled and shook his head. "True, I'm no longer with intelligence. I'm a civilian again, sent off with a handshake and certificate of merit. But they do want me to go away happy. Nothing more dangerous than a disgruntled former employee."

"Doesn't that put you in danger? I mean, don't they kill people to keep their secrets safe?"

"They're not going to kill anybody for complaining about overreach and demanding an apology. Enough of that. We've got work to do, and we don't have much time."

They both glanced at their watches. It was 4:00 p.m. "Eighteen hours until the Victory Day parade begins," he said. "I have to make a couple of phone calls, and I don't want strangers overhearing me."

"I'll take you to the apartment where I'm staying, and you can call from there. As they walked, she told him what she knew about Olga.

Olga didn't answer her door, so Nicole used her keys to let them in. She called out, but there was no answer. That's when she saw the note on the kitchen table:

> "I'm sure you and your fiancé will appreciate a little privacy. I'll be staying with a friend for a few nights, but I'll drop by during the day. By the way, I changed the sheets on the big feather bed. Enjoy!"

Nicole showed Reinhardt into Olga's office and left him to make his calls. She returned to the studio's tiny kitchen and made a cup of tea. She could hear Reinhardt's voice in the other room. It sounded as if he was giving someone a piece of his mind. Soon his voice dropped to a bare murmur. Hearing him on the phone—his tone all business—she wondered if she was a fool to believe he'd give up his old profession when he'd already failed to keep that promise once.

At last he came out of the office with his attaché case under his arm. "Put your jacket on. I didn't want to give out your friend's address, so I'm having a cab pick us up at the café where we ate. We have to stop and pick up a few things before we head over to Red Square."

As they started for the café, Reinhardt was silent, deep in thought.

"Well," she said, "When are you going to tell me where we're headed and what we're going to do?"

He looked at her, almost as if he'd forgotten she was there.

"You agreed to take over Chet's mission?" she went on. "Is that it? And I'm supposed to show you where the explosives are, right?"

"You're right, of course. I should have told you. Sorry for being such a tosser—"

"Tosser?"

He gave a little laugh. "Sometimes I forget that we don't really speak the same language. A tosser is the worst kind of asshole. Of course you need to know our plans. It's just that I'm so used to working alone. But you're right. I am taking over for Chet. They were scrambling to find a replacement, but since I turned up and the deadline is imminent, they asked if I'd do them one last favor."

He stopped talking as a couple, arm in arm, passed them going in the opposite direction. Nicole was mulling over what he'd just said. *How many last favors would his old bosses request as time went on? Was this really the last?* The thought of it chilled her until she reminded herself that she herself had asked for his help.

"Our first stop," he said, "is an establishment where they produce fake IDs and credentials. We're going to be posing as safety inspectors from the Russian Ministry of Civil Defense. Aside from the fake documents, they sell just about everything from weapons and illegal and hard-to-get goods to designer knockoffs and even tourist souvenirs.

"There are other details I need to mention—" He stopped talking as a sizeable group of pedestrians approached. He pulled Nicole through a gate into the weedy front garden of an apartment house and put his arms around her to whisper in her ear. "Sorry, but I forgot to tell you something. Aside from showing me the explosives, you have one other task."

He reached into his attaché case, took out what looked like an oversized lipstick case, and handed it to her. She looked at him questioningly.

"Inside is a thumb drive," he said. "Once we get to Red Square, your job will be to go into the office of the construction supervisor. It's a temporary structure somewhere on the square and should be easy to access. Your job is to insert the drive into his computer and download its contents."

"How will I know where to put the files?" she said. "Everything on his computer will be in Russian."

"You don't have to worry about that. The download is set to work automatically. When it's done, the drive will eject itself. The whole process shouldn't take more than a couple of minutes."

Nicole pulled back from his embrace and stared at him. "How on earth can I manage that without getting caught?"

He shushed her, pulled her back into his arms, and leaned down to whisper again. "That's my job. I'll create a diversion that will allow time for you to take care of the download while the bomb squad deals with the explosives. Then we'll make our getaway. We'll exit through an opening our team has already cut in the temporary fencing at the back of the square."

"A diversion?" she said. "What kind of diversion?"

"I'm going to plant a limited explosive device somewhere in the square. It's controlled by a trigger I'll have on my key fob. It will cause a loud explosion and a fire that's fairly limited in scope but spectacular enough to send the workers running to put it out before it spreads to the temporary structures. It contains a fire accelerant so it flames up when water hits it. That way, they won't be able to put it out until the fire trucks arrive."

"Where are you going to get this device?"

"We're being joined on this assignment by a three-member bomb demolition crew. They're picking us up when we're done shopping, and they will have the device with them. They'll walk into the square with us, carrying credentials like ours. Sorry I didn't think to clue you in on all of this. I'm so used to—"

"You're forgiven, but from now on—"

"I swear it." He put an arm around her and led her back onto the sidewalk. "Now we've worked that out, let's hurry. Our cab will be there soon." They walked quickly to the café where the cab was already waiting. After they got in, Reinhardt gave the cabbie the address, and they sped off. The trip took no more than ten minutes, leaving them off in front of a building that appeared even more derelict than Olga's apartment house. Reinhardt hit the button on the intercom next to the front door and briefly spoke into it.

A buzzer went off, and the door unlocked to admit them.

Reinhardt led Nicole into a darkened hallway and up a flight of dimly lit stairs. They walked to a door at the end of the hall and knocked. A voice from inside said something in Russian. Reinhardt answered, and the door was opened by a man dressed in a black satin dressing gown with a black-and-red print cravat. His dark hair was slicked back, which emphasized his deep widow's peak. He sported a goatee and impossibly arched eyebrows, which may have been drawn on. He looked like an actor made up to play Mephistopheles in a campy version of "Faust." He drew Reinhardt into a hug and air-kissed him on both cheeks. Only then did he notice Nicole and give her a smile.

"And who is this?" he said in accented English.

Reinhardt introduced them. The man's name was Pierre. To Nicole's great relief, she was spared the hug and kisses. Instead, he reached out to shake her hand.

"We're in a bit of a rush," Reinhardt said. "We need a few things."

"Certainly, I'll get someone to help you."

"Don't bother. I know my way around."

"Don't forget to say goodbye on your way out, my friend." Pierre patted Reinhardt's shoulder as he hurried off to answer the intercom, which was ringing again.

As Nicole followed Reinhardt inside, she was dying of curiosity. She'd never seen an establishment like this and wondered how common they were or if this one was unique. In the first room they entered, printers of various sizes were busy churning out documents. Reinhardt approached one of the workers and explained what he needed. The man handed him forms to complete. Nicole watched as Reinhardt filled in the blanks with Cyrillic. "This is for our new IDs and official papers and badges," he said. "We'll have our photos taken on our way out."

While these documents were being created, Nicole followed Reinhardt through rooms cluttered with goods of various sorts.

Each held a completely different type of inventory—icons and antiques in one room, guns and knives in another. One featured consumables, like caviar, honey, and vodka. They passed a large room overflowing with paintings and sculptures, many of which looked as if they belonged in a museum. Next came a room filled with electronic devices, including audio and video surveillance equipment, and so on. It appeared that Pierre's shop carried just about everything and took up an entire floor of the building.

They stopped at a room filled with racks of clothing and shelves of shoes piled one pair on top of another. On the wall were pictures of designer labels: Prada, Armani, Hermes, Louis Vuitton, Balenciaga, and many more. Women's apparel was on one side of the room, men's on the other.

Other shoppers were milling about, most of them clustered in what appeared to be the bridal department, a corner devoted to racks of white puffy gowns. A bridal dress, displayed on a mannequin next to the dressing room, bore a sign that said "Vera Wang" where its head should have been. Another mannequin on the opposite side of the fitting room was dressed in an orange silk, floor-length gown. This one bore a sign that said "Oscar De la Renta." The orange number was strapless, backless, and form-fitting, making a mystery of what would hold it up when it was worn on a moving body.

"Are these all knockoffs?" Nicole said.

"Every one of them. Don't be tempted by the gowns. You need clothes appropriate for an Eastern European female bureaucrat."

"I know what you mean," she said. "Serviceable but not stylish."

He nodded. "Exactly. Once you've made your choice, keep the outfit on. You'll be wearing it when we leave."

A saleswoman bustled over to help. After establishing that the saleswoman spoke no English, Reinhardt explained in Russian what Nicole needed before heading for men's clothing. He gave the attending salesman a shake of his head and waved him away. He seemed to know what he wanted and where to find it.

Nicole was happy to have someone assist her. The goods weren't organized by size but by style, and most of the clothes seemed to range from big to enormous. The saleswoman was all smiles but made no attempt to communicate verbally. Clearly, she understood that neither of them spoke the other's language. But she seemed good natured and eager to please.

Nicole chose a navy-blue suit with a belted jacket and military-looking epaulettes. It almost fit, except that she had to fold the waistband several times to raise the hemline, and this made the skirt sag in the seat. To accessorize, she chose a pair of chunky, low-heeled pumps in black suede with a matching satchel-type bag and a white silk camp shirt. The outfit certainly fit the bill. Stylish, it was not. The saleswoman left to get some wigs for Nicole to try on.

Looking around, Nicole spotted a rack of glasses and plucked out a pair of granny-style spectacles with gold rims, making sure they had clear glass lenses so they wouldn't distort her vision. Next to the glasses display was a rack of chains designed to be attached to the glasses so they could dangle around the wearer's neck when they weren't being worn. She chose a gold chain and attached it to her new glasses.

Meanwhile, the saleswoman had brought out two full, long-haired wigs, both brunette. One was curly and the other straight. Nicole tried them on and, looking in the mirror, felt utterly ridiculous. Both had way too much hair for someone as petite as she. Nicole gestured to the saleswoman that she wanted something shorter and less full. The woman went back and returned with another wig, which was slightly shorter, along with one that had braids that wrapped around it. Nicole put the braided wig on and checked the mirror. Along with the glasses, it was perfect. As long as she didn't smile and ruin the effect with her dimples, she looked like a teacher who'd be quick to whack a misbehaving student with a ruler.

When Reinhardt saw her, she could see he was trying not to laugh. But he looked almost as silly. His brown, double-breasted suit fit so poorly that the collar stood away from his neck. The jacket pulled across the chest and back because it wasn't cut for someone with broad shoulders. He was wearing a white shirt buttoned up to the top with no tie. It was a powerful contrast to his usual stylish, custom-tailored clothes. He was carrying a large, boxy briefcase. For a long moment, they took in each other's new look before they both started to laugh.

"With all these clothes to choose from, couldn't you find something that fit?" she said.

"I'm sure I could have," he said. "But this was the look I was going for. The fit of this suit is part of the strong man look I wanted. The tight jacket shows off my muscles."

"If you say so." She looked in the mirror and laughed again. What a pair they made.

Meanwhile, the saleswoman packed up the clothes they'd been wearing when they arrived. Back in the room where their documents were being prepared, they had their photos taken to be placed on their badges. The technician worked fast, and the forged credentials were soon ready. Papers, badges, and lapel pins were laid out on the table for Reinhardt's inspection. He gave his approval. Reinhardt and Nicole put on the badges and lapel pins, while the documents were neatly folded and put in an official-looking leather envelope with the Russian Republic's crest stamped in one corner.

"Charge as usual?" Pierre said.

"Yes, same account," Reinhardt said. "But this will be the last time. I won't be back. I'm moving abroad."

Pierre's face fell. Nicole suspected he was a little in love with Reinhardt, and who could blame him? "We'll miss you, my friend." He repeated the hug and air kisses. Then he gave Nicole a little bow. "Pleasure to meet you."

Transformed into Russian bureaucrats, the two of them left the building as it was getting dark. As soon as they reached the sidewalk, a shiny black stretch limo came screeching to a stop at the curb next to them. The vehicle appeared so suddenly that for the briefest moment, Nicole thought they were about to be kidnapped. Then she remembered what Reinhardt had told her about the bomb squad picking them up.

A man—short and solidly built with the typically Eastern European broad face and high cheekbones—hopped out and said something in Russian. Like Reinhardt, he was dressed in a suit, tieless, with a shirt buttoned up to the top. He was holding a substantial package wrapped in brown paper. From the careful way they both handled it, it appeared to be heavy. The driver directed Nicole and Reinhardt to the seats in the first of two back rows. In the rear row were two other men, the rest of the bomb team. As soon as they were all inside and buckled up, Reinhardt said, "Please don't start up the car until I put this away." He opened the boxy briefcase and rearranged the contents to carefully fit in the package. "Carry on," he said when he was done. The limo took off and made a tight U-turn. They were finally on their way to clean up the threat at Red Square.

Chapter Eleven

As on Nicole's previous visit to Red Square with Chet, armed guards were spread across the entryway, which was still blocked by temporary traffic barriers. Reinhardt, Nicole, and the three bomb experts walked straight for the gate, their intention clear. When they were a few feet away, the head guard thumped the butt of his rifle on the ground and shouted a command that Nicole understood to mean "Stop!" He pointed to a nearby sign, which was in Cyrillic. After glancing at the sign, Reinhardt pulled out his fake credentials and stepped forward to show them to the guard. The man ignored the documents, shaking his head and waving Reinhardt away.

The two launched into a long argument in Russian. It ended when the guard stepped back and held out the flat of his hand, signaling for Reinhardt and the others to remain where they were. Then he called over one of the other guards and sent him into the square.

Reinhardt turned to Nicole and explained in a low voice. "He says no one is to be admitted except the workers finishing up. No exceptions. He's sent one of his men to get the construction supervisor who, he says, will tell me the same thing. Don't worry. We've got this covered."

After a few minutes, the guard came back with a burly man wearing a hard hat. His clothes—trousers held up with suspenders and a white shirt with the sleeves rolled up—were rumpled as if he'd been sleeping in them. He seemed thoroughly annoyed and ready for a fight. Perhaps he'd been asleep or interrupted at a bad moment. Maybe he was ill-tempered by nature. He and Reinhardt had a long argument, during which Reinhardt kept trying to hand the man his papers with no better luck than he'd had with the guard. Nicole could see that this man, just like the guard, was determined to not let them in and didn't give a damn about what credentials they had.

Finally, Reinhardt pulled out his phone and tapped in a number. Someone answered, Reinhardt spoke briefly then handed the phone to the supervisor. As the man listened, his expression changed from belligerent to nervous and even a little abashed. He seemed cowed by the person on the other end. He muttered "Da" a few times before he handed the phone back. He immediately moved the temporary barrier aside and waved them into the square.

The phone call had completely changed his attitude. As he escorted the group into the square, his manner was polite and even hospitable. But it was soon clear that he wasn't planning to let them roam his building site on their own. Instead, he assumed the role of host and guide. As they walked along, he introduced himself as Vlad Galyorkin. This much Nicole understood, but the rest of his chatter was lost on her.

Reinhardt introduced Nicole and the bomb experts to Vlad. Dmitry was their driver. The other two were Ilya, and Vadim. All had last names that were too long and complicated for Nicole to catch.

She'd been too distracted by Reinhardt's efforts to get into the square to give them a close look when they got out of the van. They made an interesting group. They all had facial hair. Dmitry sported a square mustache just under his nose. Ilya had a well-trimmed goatee and handlebar mustache. He was wearing gray sweats with a hoodie. Vadim, tall and broad-chested, had a beard and mustache that were so thick and unruly that his mouth was barely visible. Nicole wondered what happened when he ate. He was wearing a heavy black overcoat. The three of them followed along silently, contributing as little to the conversation as Nicole.

As they walked, the supervisor chattered on, pointing to each new structure they passed. He was obviously proud of the project and his role in supervising its construction. Reinhardt and the others paid scant attention. They stopped repeatedly to do the job they were purportedly here for—inspect the bleachers and other temporary buildings. They looked each one over carefully, taking time to check beneath and behind the structures.

At several points, workmen appeared, apparently wanting to ask the supervisor a question. He was visibly annoyed when they approached and impatiently waved them away. When one man persisted, Vlad thumped his ear with a fist and yelled, letting the man know he was too busy to be bothered. After he sent each worker scampering away, Vlad would turn back to Reinhardt and the others, once more the genial host.

Before they arrived, Nicole and Reinhardt had discussed what she could do to disguise the fact that she didn't know Russian. If anyone addressed her, they decided, she'd pretend she had laryngitis. She'd practiced pointing to her throat and make a croaking sound until she was satisfied she could pull it off.

Even though she didn't understand what they were saying, Nicole found it interesting to watch the interaction between Reinhardt and Vlad. Vlad was overly polite and deferential, as if he were talking to someone not just important but to be feared. Reinhardt, on the other hand, appeared dismissive, making it clear he was barely listening to the man. His expression was serious, even grim, as if he expected to find building violations and other problems with the new construction. He appeared intent on the inspection and wasn't going to let Vlad distract him.

This reminded Nicole of the first time she met Reinhardt, when he was investigating a major drug ring. She'd found him sinister and more than a little frightening. At the time, she hadn't known he was with the police.

As the minutes ticked off and it was clear Vlad wasn't going to leave, Nicole grew more anxious. How were they going to complete their mission under his watchful eyes? When they'd gone halfway along the row of bleachers, they were almost even with the grandstand. Nicole moved closer to Reinhardt and bumped her hip against his so he'd look at her. She tipped her head in the direction of the grandstand. Behind the stand, Lenin's tomb had disappeared under a giant toaster-shaped cover decorated with Russian flags and some kind of motto in Cyrillic. Reinhardt nodded his understanding that the grandstand was where the explosives were hidden.

He immediately stepped closer to Vlad and spoke to him. The man nodded, pointed back the way they'd come, and appeared to be giving Reinhardt directions. Before he set off, Reinhardt turned to wink at Nicole and hurried off in the direction Vlad had pointed.

Nicole was pretty sure what that wink meant. Reinhardt had asked where the toilets were, but that wasn't where he was headed. Like her, he must have realized they were never going to get rid of Vlad, so he was going straight to the planned diversion. She thought of the thumb drive he'd given her and wondered how she was supposed to install it on Vlad's computer when she had no idea where his office was. Nor did she know how to find the gap in the fence that was supposed to be their escape route. She'd assumed Reinhardt would point these places out to her, but he hadn't had a chance. Vlad's presence had undermined their carefully orchestrated plan.

She was still wondering what to do when, to her great relief, Reinhardt reappeared, and she realized she'd been mistaken.

He must have planted the diversionary device but was going to wait until later to set it off. Shortly after resuming their walk, Reinhardt tapped Nicole's arm with his elbow and tilted his head toward a path between two sections of the bleachers. Here it is; he was signaling the way out.

The group continued toward the rear of the square. Vlad was walking on Reinhardt's other side, talking nonstop. Although she couldn't understand him, Nicole could tell he was still bragging about what he'd achieved here. She wondered what hours he kept. It was already past 8:00 p.m., and he was still here. Now that she thought about it, his clothes looked as if he'd slept in them. Maybe he was here twenty-four hours a day, catching some sleep in his office when he had the chance. The parade was the next morning, and, while the square appeared almost ready, there was still work to do.

At the end of the bleachers, Vlad stopped the group in front of a small temporary building, which turned out to be his office. The door was standing open. Perhaps he'd made sure his workers were so terrified of him that they wouldn't dare enter without his permission.

Vlad yawned and gave a big stretch before putting a hand on Reinhardt's shoulder and waving him inside. Vlad then turned to Nicole and the three others and pointed to a make-shift canteen nearby, where they could get coffee and a snack. Reinhardt took Vlad aside and, gesturing toward Nicole, seemed to be explaining something. Vlad looked at Nicole, then back at Reinhardt and smiled, pointing to each of them and nodding his head approvingly. Reinhardt nodded back. Clearly, he'd told the supervisor that he and Nicole were a couple, so she'd be invited into the office, too. Sure enough, Vlad waved her in. Once they were inside, he said something to her that was clearly a question. She pointed to her throat, and Reinhardt answered for her, explaining she had laryngitis. Nicole understood the next thing

Vlad said because the Russian word was the same as it was in English.

"Vodka!" Vlad reached for a bottle on a table top. He filled three tumblers half full and handed one to Nicole, another to Reinhardt. Both men drank theirs in a single gulp. Nicole took a sip. The vodka was harsh and burned her throat. She held onto the glass, figuring she could dump the remaining vodka in the trash can next to her when the others were looking the other way. Vlad motioned Reinhardt over to his computer, eager to show it off. It had a large screen and looked brand new.

He'd just put in his password when there was a knock at the open door. They all turned to see one of the workers standing there. He had a smile on his face and was carrying two bottles of vodka, obviously intended for his boss. Vlad got up from his chair, glanced at the bottles, then back at the man. He appeared extremely displeased—whether by the interruption or the brand of vodka was unclear. He shouted and shoved the man out of the office so he landed hard on the stone pavement, surrounded by shards of glass from the broken bottles. Nicole was thinking what a misery it would be to work for Vlad, but she'd heard that Russians respected strong men, the kind who mistreated their underlings.

Vlad went back to his computer and typed something in. A blueprint of one of the bleachers popped up.

While Vlad was occupied, Reinhardt reached into his pocket and started fiddling with his keys. Nicole braced herself for the explosion. It came a moment later, a huge blast that shook the ground. Vlad dashed outside. Reinhardt waited until he disappeared, then leaned close and whispered, "When you're done with the download, wait outside for ten minutes, no more. If I'm not back, leave through the gap in the fence. A car will be along to pick you up." He hurried out, turning in the same direction Vlad had taken.

Nicole got the thumb drive out of her purse and went to work. Fortunately, Vlad had already put in his password, so she didn't have to worry about that. She inserted the thumb drive into the computer. While it was downloading, she peeked outside to see what was going on. The flames and billows of smoke were coming from the row of portable toilet booths that Vlad had pointed out earlier to Reinhardt. They were at the opposite end of the square. The area near Vlad's office was deserted. Everyone had run to put out the flames before they spread to the newly built bleachers, which were made of wood and highly flammable.

When she turned back to the computer, the download was complete. She ejected the drive and put it in her purse. After making sure the computer was just as Vlad had left it, she went outside to wait for Reinhardt. The entire row of portable toilets was on fire, although it hadn't spread beyond them. Men were throwing buckets of water on the flames. Instead of putting them out, the water seemed to be feeding the fire, which was burning furiously. The sound of sirens split the air as several fire trucks arrived. Men jumped off, readied their hoses, and went about spraying foam on the flames, which quickly put them out.

Nicole checked her watch. It was time to leave. Just then, she spotted Reinhardt hurrying toward her. He gestured for her to follow, then headed back along the rows of bleachers. She had to run to keep up with his long strides.

"We're going back to the speaker's stand," he said.

"But why?"

"I've decided it would be best to wait until the police arrive so I have a chance to talk to them. After Vlad is arrested, we'll disappear."

Before she could ask why Vlad would be arrested and what it had to do with them, they'd reached the grandstand. The three bomb experts were talking to several uniformed policemen and gesturing toward the entrance to the stand's underside. Dmitri handed a cop one of the fake cinderblocks, while Ilya held out the toolbox that had been sitting in front of the pyramid of explosives.

Moments later, three more officers arrived with Vlad close behind. He was talking in a loud voice, apparently desperate to explain something to them. Reinhardt stepped forward, flashed his credentials for the police to see, and spoke to them, pointing first at Vlad then in the direction of his office. The cops grabbed Vlad and pulled him toward it. He resisted, protesting angrily. Reinhardt and Nicole followed until they were within sight of Vlad's office. Here Reinhardt stopped and grabbed Nicole's arm.

In a low voice, he said, "We're going to wait until the police take Vlad into his office. The thumb drive left evidence on his computer implicating him in planting the explosives. It also left messages that indicate he was conspiring with others. They'll arrest him and take his computer. Before they get around to questioning us, we'll be gone."

Nicole blinked. Vlad was going to meet a horrible fate. She would have felt sorrier for him if he hadn't been so abusive to his underlings. The reality was that someone had to be blamed for planting the explosives. Having it be a Russian was preferable to implicating the real culprits, the Ukrainian dissidents, considering what the fallout would be. It appeared that they were going to walk away from this without paying for what they'd done. They hadn't succeeded in blowing up the parade, but they had conspired to do it, and they'd murdered Derek Swan for reasons that were still unclear.

As the police dragged Vlad into his office, an announcement came over the loudspeakers. It must have mentioned a second bomb threat because workers ran for the exit. Reinhardt steered Nicole quickly in the opposite direction, leading her to the place where the fence had been cut. Meanwhile, more police cars were arriving, along with a truck hauling a heavy, six-wheeled vehicle with a robotic arm. This had to be Moscow's bomb squad, although the cinder-block explosives had been rendered harmless once the toolbox with the igniting mechanism was removed.

Nicole and Reinhardt squeezed through the hole in the fence and onto a side street. The street was blocked from the main boulevard with traffic barriers. "A van was supposed to be waiting," Reinhardt said. He walked to the end of the street where barriers were blocking access and moved one of them aside.

Nicole followed him. "I don't understand," she said. "If Vlad is being arrested, why do we have to run?"

"The cops will want to talk to us. We don't want them looking closely at our papers. It's too big a risk they'll figure out they're forgeries. And they'll quickly realize you can't be a ministry employee if you don't even speak Russian." He looked up and down the street for the missing van. "We'd better take cover. They'll be looking for us."

Just then the van pulled up to the curb next to them. Dmitri was at the wheel and the two others in back. As Nicole and Reinhardt were climbing in, a police car arrived at the intersection. The van started up, turned onto the main boulevard, and quickly joined the flow of traffic, but it was too late. The police must have noticed that the traffic barrier had been moved and realized the van shouldn't have been on a street next to Red Square that had been blocked for security reasons. The van sped up with the squad car close behind. Dmitri went faster, turning corners in an attempt to lose the police. There was a loud cracking sound, and Nicole realized they'd shot out the back window. Except for Dmitri, everyone in the van ducked down in anticipation of another round of fire. At the next corner, he pushed the gas pedal to the floor. The van made a screeching turn, then another, veering down a steep driveway into an underground garage. He pressed a button on the visor and the gate to the garage closed behind him. Nicole looked back in time to catch sight of the police car passing the entrance. The police must have arrived at the last turn too late to see them enter the garage.

Dmitri drove to the bottom level and parked. He gestured for everyone to get out and tossed a set of car keys to Reinhardt, pointing to a parking spot with a Russian-made sedan badly in need of a wash. Then Dmitri led his two companions to an old Volvo hatchback. Reinhardt and Nicole got in the small sedan and waited for Dmitri and the others to start up the ramp before following.

As they headed away, they could hear sirens. Squad cars, fire trucks, and maybe ambulances were still arriving at the explosion site.

CHAPTER TWELVE

"ARE WE GOING BACK TO OLGA'S?" Nicole said, as Reinhardt drove from the garage into the street.

He turned to look at her. "I'm not sure that's a good idea. We look out of place in that neighborhood, and the last thing we want to do is raise suspicion. Of course, a harmless old woman's apartment could be a safe hiding place—"

Nicole interrupted. "Who said she's harmless? She makes a habit of helping dissidents and people in trouble with the police. That's why she took me in. I think she may be part of some kind of underground organization." Nicole explained how Abby, the reporter, had immediately thought of Olga as someone who'd give her a place to hide.

"What's Olga's last name?" he said.

"That's an interesting question. Abby never told me and neither did Olga. I got the feeling she doesn't want anyone to know. But I found a letter when I was looking through her bookshelves. It was addressed to Olga Marozova."

His eyebrows shot up. "Olga Whitney Marozova? She's famous! An American heiress who defected to Russia, grew disillusioned with the Communists, and became an anti-Soviet activist. She was briefly married to one of our agents, Nikolas Marozov."

"Marozov? Her name is Marozova."

"Marozova is the feminine form of Marozov. Later on, your

Olga was arrested by the KGB and locked up. I had the impression she died in prison. What did the letter say? And don't pretend you didn't read it."

Nicole smiled. "You know me so well. It was a letter from a rejected suitor named Max. He didn't sign his last name. Apparently, Olga wasn't interested. She's in her seventies now, I'm guessing, but she's still attractive under that turban and all the heavy clothes she wears to bulk herself out. She did mention that she was once married to a spy. She didn't like his constant disappearances, so she gave him an ultimatum. He could be her husband or continue working for MI6. Does that sound familiar?"

"Nicole, I swear—"

She started to say she'd been joking, then changed her mind. "You did go missing for all those months after you promised to join me in a week. So, how do I know—?"

"I explained all that, and I thought you understood. But you still don't trust me, do you?"

"How can I? You said you were done spying, and now here you are again."

"That's not fair. I only took this on because you needed my help. Besides, the agency promised to get you safely out of Russia if I did it."

Somewhat mollified, she said, "I know. I did ask for your help, so it's ridiculous to criticize you for it. I do love you, and I want this to work out. But it worries me. What if you can't find a satisfying job? What if you feel trapped and miss your old life? You'll start to resent me. Our relationship—or our marriage, if we get that far—will fall apart."

"What more can I say except that I'm done with all that? You can't imagine how much I longed for you these past months. All I want is a future with you—a normal life, a family."

She shrugged and looked out the window as a tear made its way down her cheek. "We'll have to wait and see, won't we?

Anyway, back to Marozov. He couldn't bring himself to—what do you call it—come in from the cold? So they split. Olga's still pretty bitter about it."

"You know, Marozov was a legend at the agency, one of the most successful double agents we ever had."

Nicole took note of the admiration in his voice. He still identified with MI6. Any fool could see that. Was he really ready to make the break? Now that her doubts had surfaced again, it was hard to shake them.

A long, uneasy silence passed before he spoke again. "The agency has several safe houses here in Moscow. I think that would be our best bet."

"Good," she said. "But I want to stop at Olga's first. I want to give her back the outfit she lent me and pick up the things I left there. I also want to thank her and say goodbye. Why don't you drop me off a block away? I'll get my stuff and come right back."

Nicole gave him Olga's address. He pulled over to check his phone for directions and took off again.

Starting up the stairs of the old building, she could hear loud voices from above. The dominant one was Olga's. She was speaking Russian, but Nicole could tell the woman was angry and protesting. Meanwhile several male voices tried unsuccessfully to interrupt her tirade.

Nicole climbed faster, thinking she might be able to help. She soon reached the point in the stairs where she could see Olga and three male visitors who looked like police detectives. They seemed to be insisting Olga let them in. The door, open just a crack, was secured with a chain lock.

When Nicole reached the landing for Olga's apartment, the woman's eyes rested on her momentarily and quickly looked away. Her expression made it clear that she wasn't going to acknowledge Nicole and didn't want her involved in whatever was going on. Nicole continued up the stairs until she couldn't be seen but could still hear them. The argument continued several more minutes until Olga's door slammed shut. The men could be heard talking as they trotted down the stairs. Nicole waited a bit to be sure they were gone before she returned to Olga's apartment and tapped lightly on the door. There was no response. She knocked louder. Nothing inside stirred. Either Olga was in the other room and couldn't hear, or she wasn't answering because she was afraid the men had come back.

Nicole still had the keys to the apartment. She wasn't going to let herself in knowing Olga was inside, refusing to answer. Instead, she slid them under the door and hurried down the stairs. Her thoughts were on Olga, hoping she was safe. That the woman had been visited by the police was a bad sign. On the other hand, they could have easily broken the chain lock if they were determined to search the apartment or arrest her, but they hadn't. She knew Olga had another place to stay and hoped she'd go there and remain until whatever it was blew over. Most of all, she hoped that she herself hadn't somehow brought this trouble to Olga's door.

Heading back to the car, Nicole realized she was never going to be able to return Olga's lovely dress and fur jacket or get her own things back. She didn't care about the clothes she'd left, which weren't even hers. But she did regret the loss of her Kate Spade bag, the only designer purse she'd ever owned.

Reinhardt was waiting in the car just as she'd left him. After she got in, she told him what had been going on at Olga's.

"Don't worry too much about Olga," he said. "She may be in trouble, but she's a survivor. If this is a serious threat, she'll figure a way out. She's a bit like you in that way. Now buckle up. I've found us a place to stay."

The safe house was in an elegant old building. From what Nicole could see in the dark, it appeared to be a classical-style mansion converted into apartments. She'd read about such buildings in her guidebook. They dated back to the nineteenth century, long before the Communists came into power. The lobby had lost whatever grandeur it might have had. In front of the bronze door of the elevator was a sign in Cyrillic.

"Out of order," Reinhardt translated.

They looked up at the circular staircase with its worn carpet. Nicole was so tired, she wanted to lie down on one of the faded velvet-covered benches in the lobby. But Reinhardt took her arm, and they climbed the stairs. Their suite was on the second of three floors.

The living room was in amazing shape compared with the rest of the building. Its décor included a huge chandelier and a large gilt-framed mirror that reflected itself over and over in an identical mirror on the opposite wall. The rest of the room featured panels of verdant landscapes that appeared to have been applied directly to the walls. The furnishings had a pink and white motif: white walls and carpeting with one pink sofa flanked by two white ones. Three white stools stood in front of the couch arrangement, each topped with a fuchsia cushion.

Nicole stood in the doorway taking it in. "This is one of the prettiest places I've ever stayed in."

"With these safe houses, you never know what you're going to get," Reinhardt said. "It could be something like this or a dank basement with primitive plumbing and a wood-burning stove." He took off his coat and tossed it on one of the couches. Nicole did the same. She found a store of new toothbrushes in the bathroom as well as small tubes of toothpaste. After brushing her teeth, she took a quick shower. Lacking pj's or a robe, she wrapped herself in a towel and got into bed. Reinhardt disappeared into the bathroom, and she dozed off to the sound of the running shower.

She half woke when she felt him get into bed. He put his arms around her. "Are you asleep?"

"Not quite."

"Are you totally knackered?"

She turned and wrapped herself around him so their arms and legs intertwined. "Maybe not completely."

§

When Nicole woke up, she was alone in bed. She dressed in the things she'd worn the day before and went into the living room. Reinhardt was sitting on one of the couches, talking on the phone.

She went through an arched doorway and found herself in a huge dining room with a mahogany table and twelve matching chairs. Another turn and she was in a tiny galley kitchen. It appeared to have been recently remodeled with new appliances but minimally equipped—just an oven, cooktop, and small refrigerator. A toaster and microwave were sitting on the counter. She found coffee and strawberry jam in the refrigerator, a loaf of bread and butter in the freezer. She poked around in the cupboards until she located an electric kettle and a French press coffee pot. When the coffee was ready, she brought a cup to Reinhardt, who was still on the phone, speaking in Russian.

She mouthed "toast" to him. But he shook his head and pointed to the phone, indicating he'd be a while. She assumed he was arranging to get them out of the country. On her way back to the kitchen, she looked around more carefully and noticed the place didn't have a TV. She wondered how they were going to keep themselves informed. Hoping to find a morning paper, she opened the front door and found that two had been delivered. One was in Russian, but the second, to her delight, was a copy of today's *International New York Times*. She took it with her back to the kitchen, made herself buttered toast with jam, then carried the coffee, toast, and papers into the dining room, where she settled at the table.

Reinhardt was on the phone a good while. When he finally hung up, he passed through the dining room on his way to the kitchen, stopping to kiss the top of her head before moving on. He returned with the coffee pot and poured her another cup before ducking back into the kitchen to make his toast.

When he sat down at the table, she unfolded the Russian newspaper. It had a banner headline with a several photos of previous years' military parades, marking the day's celebration. After glancing at the pictures, Nicole passed the paper to Reinhardt. "Does this have anything about what happened last night?"

He pushed his plate aside to leaf through the paper then shook his head. "No word of it, and I'm not surprised. The Russian government wouldn't allow a story like that to appear. It would make their security apparatus for today's celebration look bad— an explosion, fire, and the arrest of the construction supervisor for planting a bomb under Putin's seat. You can bet Putin will be told, and heads will roll. I'll bet one of his body doubles will be standing in for him today."

"Were you able to arrange transportation home?"

"Indeed, I was. I'm afraid it's fairly roundabout, so it will take us a while to get to our plane. We have to avoid Moscow's three international terminals. They'll have people on high alert looking for you."

"I thought I was going to change my appearance again and get a new fake ID."

"You are. Even so, it isn't worth the risk. That's why we're waiting until tonight before we leave. We need time to get your new documents, and we're going to order a few things from Pierre's store. I'll take your photo and email it to him so his people can make you a new passport. You'll need something to wear. That suit—" He shook his head.

She looked down at the suit. After only a day's wear, it was wrinkled and the fabric had developed tiny fuzzballs. "You mean, you don't like it? I've become rather fond of it. And what about you? Do you get a new identity, too?"

He gave a chuckle. "No need. My attaché case has several fake IDs and passports in a hidden compartment. Here's what you'll need for the flight: a fashionable coat, expensive-looking boots, a designer bag, and a wig to complete your disguise. Keep in mind that we're supposed to look like people who can afford to hire a private jet. I'm ordering a new overcoat. My own has taken quite a beating the last few months." He didn't elaborate, and she knew better than to ask.

"Here's the plan," he went on. "A car and driver will pick us up in the garage downstairs around 7:30 this evening. He'll drop us at a small, private dock on the Volga, just north of Moscow. A cabin cruiser will come for us. We'll follow the river to Yaroslavl. From there we'll be taken by limo to a small airport. A private jet will be waiting. All customs red tape has been cleared, so our driver can deliver us directly to the plane. We'll fly to Helsinki. From there, we'll pick up a commercial flight."

"But first we're going to Pierre's again?"

"I'm afraid it's not safe for you to leave this building until our driver picks us up tonight. Pierre suggested you look at some online clothing sites, pick examples of what you want, and send him an email with the links."

"Does this apartment have a computer so I can look for things?" She wouldn't admit it to anyone, especially Reinhardt, but online shopping was one of her favorite pastimes. The prospect made her feel newly energized.

"Righto," he said. "They've got one hidden 'round here somewhere. Be sure to send Pierre several options for each item, along with your size. He'll have a saleswoman find something similar. As for the wig, pick a different color."

"Red?" she speculated. "No, that would be too attention grabbing. Maybe auburn."

He didn't answer. She could tell he was deeply absorbed in the article he was reading. After a moment, he pushed away his plate with the half-eaten toast.

"Listen to this." He read the story aloud, translating as he went along:

> Seven Ukrainian nationals posing as American tourists were arrested and removed from the river cruise ship *Queen of the Volga* when it docked in St. Petersburg. They were charged with drug running and the murder of a tourist while the ship was docked in Moscow, the starting point of the cruise.
>
> Another passenger had already been detained as a conspirator in the murder. The seven arrested in St. Petersburg are being sent back to Moscow for trial."

Reinhardt looked up at her. "And they'll be shown no mercy from Russia's justice system."

"So they didn't walk away free after all," Nicole said. "But why would they be charged with drug trafficking?"

"Maybe that was a sideline of theirs. Or Russian authorities found out about their planned attack on Red Square and didn't want the public to know the plot almost succeeded. By the way, the big military parade begins—" he paused to glance at his watch. "—in fifty-five minutes."

Nicole was quiet a long moment, considering this before something else occurred to her. "What would their motive have been for killing Swan? Any thoughts?"

"It's possible he was a covert operative, and they were on to him."

"But if there was already a spy in the group, why was I recruited to keep an eye on them? I don't get it."

"The U.K. isn't the only country with covert operatives. He might have been from Denmark—or the States, for that matter. Here, let me find the computer. We should get our orders in to

Pierre as soon as possible."

He went over to a large cabinet standing against the wall. After removing several stacks of bowls and platters, he crouched in front of it and peered inside. Finally, he slid a rear panel over and pulled out a laptop computer.

"How did you know where it was? Have you been here before?"

"No, but there's a pattern to how these places are set up. Generally, you'll find the electronics in a dining room closet or cabinet. If there's no dining room, the place to look is in a kitchen cupboard near the refrigerator. He plugged the computer into an outlet near where Nicole was seated and placed it in front of her. Then he typed in a password and went back to reading the paper.

She spent a happy hour choosing an outfit, coat, boots, wig, and underwear. Reinhardt jotted down Pierre's email address and handed it to her while she was working on her order. When she was done, she wrote Pierre a message that included links to her choices, along with her sizes. After sending off the message, she poured them each more coffee before settling down to finish reading the paper.

She felt completely disconnected from the news back home—congressional infighting, growing protests over grievances she was usually sympathetic to; op-ed columnists' predictions of inflation, deflation, or a looming depression; fresh alarms about the fate of the earth; reviews of plays, movies, TV shows. It all seemed impossibly distant, as if it were covering life on another planet. She'd scan the beginning of one story and move on to the next.

Reinhardt interrupted her thoughts. "Why don't you take a nap this afternoon? Last night was exhausting, and we'll be up 'til all hours tonight."

"What about you?"

"It depends on when the clothes we ordered are ready. I have to pick them up."

"Don't they deliver?"

"Of course, but I can't give this address to anyone. I'll probably go after lunch."

She moved to the couch, put her feet up, and used the laptop to continue the Margaret Atwood book she'd been reading at Olga's. Reinhardt spent the rest of the morning on the phone in the bedroom with the door closed.

She figured he was planning the details of their exit or, perhaps, debriefing their exploit in Red Square the previous evening. She was just starting to feel hungry when Reinhardt emerged from the bedroom. "Sorry. Got caught up in logistics."

"It's time for lunch. But all we have is bread and jam."

"We'll call in an order to a restaurant I noticed down the street," he said. He gave her the name of the restaurant. She looked it up online. Reading over her shoulder, he translated the menu. She decided on pierogi, which she'd never had, and hot borscht with meat and vegetables. If this was to be her last day here, she might as well have a thoroughly Russian meal.

Reinhardt added his order and left. He was soon back with two bags of food and a bottle of wine tucked under his arm. He put everything on the table while Nicole set it. When they were done eating, there were enough leftovers for dinner. While she packed it up and put it in the refrigerator, Reinhardt called Pierre to see if their order was ready. When he hung up, he said, "It's almost complete. If I leave now, it will be done by the time I get there." He kissed her goodbye and grabbed his coat on the way out.

Nicole picked up the laptop and returned to her book. About an hour later, she heard a knock at the door. She jumped up and started toward it, thinking Reinhardt must be back. Then she realized he wouldn't have knocked. He had a key. She tiptoed silently to the peephole and looked out. Her hunch had been right. It wasn't Reinhardt standing there. It was Colonel Kolkov. She stepped away and stood with her back to the door, afraid to breathe. How could he possibly know she was here? He must have followed them and waited in the garage hoping Reinhardt would leave before he approached the apartment.

Kolkov gave up knocking and started banging on the door. "Open door," he shouted. "Open or I shoot out lock!"

Nicole went into the bedroom and pulled Reinhardt's bulky briefcase out of the closet. A rolled-up black polyester garment of some kind filled most of the case. She tossed it aside and located the concealed bottom compartment Reinhardt had mentioned. It contained several passports, some papers, and a gun. She recognized it as a semi-automatic pistol, a Glock 20, which was at least twice the size of the small revolver she owned. She'd never handled a semi-automatic, much less a weapon as big as this, but she didn't have a choice. She was an excellent shot and figured she'd just have to manage the extra weight and brace herself for the weapon's recoil.

Nicole rushed back through the apartment, passing into the dining room just as an explosive bang rang out, then another and another as Kolkov made good his threat to shoot out the lock. With a crash, the doorknob fell onto the floor. She flattened herself against the wall by the doorway to the living room. The hinges squeaked as the front door was pushed open. She raised the gun and got ready to fire. She could hear floorboards creaking as Kolkov entered. Otherwise the building was completely silent. Where were the other residents? Hadn't they heard the shots? Why hadn't they come out to see what was going on?

Kolkov called her name, then muttered to himself before shouting, "I know you're here. I saw man friend go. Police department talk demotion, even firing if I don't bring you in— what you Americans say?—dead or alive. In your case, I say dead. Then you can't escape." He was working his way around the living room.

She briefly leaned forward and caught sight of him looking

behind one of the couches. He had his gun out, ready to shoot. Before she could take aim, he was on the move again. She pressed herself back against the wall. There was a silence, and she figured he must be searching the bedroom and bathroom. Moments later, the floor creaked again as he moved through the living room.

Only as he started to enter the dining room did he sense her presence. Before he could swing around and shoot, she pulled the trigger. The bullet hit his forehead. Blood spattered out in an arc behind him, as he staggered backward. His gun went off as he fell onto the living room floor. His shot narrowly missed the chandelier, bringing down a shower of plaster.

He lay still in a pool of blood, although it no longer was pouring from his head. Nicole waited a long moment before approaching. She made sure there was no visible rise and fall of his chest to indicate he was still breathing. She kicked his gun out of the way before bending down to check his pulse. There was none.

She closed the front door. Anyone passing by would surely notice that the lock had been shot open, but at least they wouldn't be able to see Kolkov's dead body on the floor. She sank onto one of the couches and tried not to look at him. She kept thinking of the terrible moment the bullet hit and blood exploded from his head.

Why did these things keep happening to her? Like the other times, this was self-defense. Kolkov had broken in with the full intention of killing her. But that was little comfort. She'd been forced to take another human life. Over the last few years, she'd accumulated a high enough body count to qualify as a serial killer. What was wrong with her that she kept finding herself in these situations?

It felt like forever before Reinhardt returned. He kicked the door open, his gun drawn. "Nicole," he called. "Where are—" he went silent when he saw the body and froze for a moment before turning to close the door. Nicole was sitting on the couch with the gun still in her hands. She looked at him. "That's the police detective who arrested me. Somehow he followed us here and broke in after you left. He had his gun out and was going to kill me. I pulled the trigger first." She glanced at the body and quickly looked away. "What are we going to do?"

He took the gun from her, wiped it with a handkerchief he pulled from his pocket, and set it on the coffee table. "Don't worry. I'll make a call. We have people who'll come in, get rid of the body, and clean up. But we'll have to leave before they arrive." After going back out to the hall where he'd left the garment bags and packages from Pierre's, he brought them in, locking the door behind him.

"What about the neighbors?" Nicole said. "Wouldn't they have heard the shots? Are they all cowering in their apartments?"

"The building is empty. It was designated a cultural landmark and slated to be restored as a museum, but they've never gotten around to it."

She didn't bother asking how MI6 was allowed to maintain an apartment here. The agency worked in mysterious ways.

"Don't worry. Everything will be taken care of," he said. "You need to change, but first you'd best take a shower. While you're getting ready, I'll call and get someone out here."

He handed her several of the bags he was holding, and she headed for the bathroom to shower. She felt sick. At the same time, she had a weird sensation, as if she were moving in slow motion. She recognized this as shock.

She looked in the mirror. There was blood on her clothes, some spattered on her hands and arms even though she had no recollection of touching Kolkov or the blood pooled around his head. She attributed this to shock. Shuddering with horror, she quickly stripped and stepped into the shower. When she was clean, she bundled the soiled clothes in a towel, which she put in a plastic laundry bag she found under the sink. She tossed it in the tub and hurriedly put on her new outfit—a skirt and blouse of some kind, which she barely looked at.

When she came out of the bathroom, Reinhardt was dressed in slacks and a blue shirt, over which he wore a black polyester vest. She recognized it as the item she'd seen in his briefcase. It had a deep V neckline so it wouldn't be visible under a jacket.

"What's that you're wearing?" she said. "A bulletproof vest?"

"No, but it is waterproof. As I said, part of our trip to the plane is by boat, and you never know what's going to happen. This way, I don't have to worry about losing my attaché case. I can leave it behind and carry my weapon and passports in my pockets. Give me your new passport and I'll stow it with mine."

He put on the new sports jacket and overcoat from Pierre's shop. He gestured toward the bed where he'd laid out Nicole's new coat and high-heeled boots. The coat was stunning, made of a dark green velvety fabric with a black fur collar. When she picked it up and put it on, she was surprised to discover it was lined with the black fur. It felt wonderfully warm and soft.

"Are you all right?" Reinhardt said. She nodded, and he put his arms around her. "You're still shaking, but everything is going to be fine. You did the right thing."

When she nodded, he released her and headed for the door. "Well then, let's go down to the garage and wait for our car and driver. Unfortunately, he isn't due for another three hours. Is there anything else you want to bring?"

"This is all I need," she said, lifting the bag from Pierre's. The cosmetics and wig for her makeover were inside. "I can tend to my makeup and the rest in the car. How on earth did he find us?"

"I have no idea, but we have to be extremely careful that no one follows us this time. Come on. We need to get out of here."

CHAPTER THIRTEEN

NICOLE AND REINHARDT WENT DOWN to the garage to wait for their ride that would take them on the first leg of their journey. Reinhardt unlocked the car they'd arrived in so they could sit while they waited. She emptied the contents of the bag she was carrying into her lap and turned the sun visor to the other side, where a vanity mirror was mounted. The mirror was small and the lighting poor. She could only hope her efforts would make her look convincingly different than herself.

Just then, a paneled truck entered the garage. Both of them turned to watch as it parked and four men got out. Their jumpsuits identified them as workmen. They opened the back doors of the van and unloaded janitorial tools—mops, a broom, and several buckets filled with brushes, rags, and cleaning products. The last item they pulled out of the truck was a rolled-up tarp. Nicole was pretty sure it would be used to wrap Kolkov's body so they could take it away. They were here to get rid of all traces of his death. Loaded down with equipment, they headed for the door to the lobby.

"Is that our cleanup crew?" Nicole said, although she was pretty sure she knew the answer.

"Right. They were quick getting here. Sorry we're stuck so long waiting for our ride."

They talked a bit, then cuddled up to listen to lively Russian music on some CDs she found in the glove compartment. When they grew tired of sitting, they got out and walked around. Nicole had a feeling their ride wasn't going to show up at all, and they'd be left to their own devices.

Three and a half hours passed before a car entered the garage. It was a black Mercedes sedan with darkened back windows. The driver was wearing a black suit and a chauffeur's cap. Nicole and Reinhardt climbed into the back seat. No greetings were exchanged, no introductions made. Reinhardt didn't appear to find this odd, although Nicole did. But she supposed this was how coverts operated. The less known, the better.

The car exited the garage and negotiated the adjacent streets until it merged onto a major highway. It was obvious the driver knew exactly where he was taking them. Reinhardt and Nicole spoke in low voices, while the driver maintained his silence. After about a half hour, the turn light indicator started clicking. The car sped down an offramp and turned left to go through an underpass. Within a few minutes, they entered the grounds of a large, castle-like house built of stone. The car drove up to it then, without slowing, continued around to the rear. The long driveway led down to the river, where a speedboat was waiting at the dock.

It was getting dark. Nicole checked her watch. It was 8:30 p.m. She waited while Reinhardt shook hands with the driver and handed him an envelope. She could only guess what was in it—a tip perhaps or some kind of report.

She looked up at the big house. All the drapes were pulled closed, and it looked deserted. The boat waiting for them, a cabin cruiser, wasn't as big as she'd expected. The cabin was small. Behind it, a deck was just big enough for four seats. The pilot got out to greet them. Once again, no names were exchanged. The man looked at Nicole and said, "Is this the critical asset we're delivering to the airfield?" Reinhardt nodded, while Nicole, who disliked being talked about as if she weren't there, flashed the man a dimpled smile and bobbed an ironic curtsy. Reinhardt chuckled, while the pilot just looked puzzled.

He suggested they sit behind him on the small bench in the cabin instead of taking the roomier chairs on the back deck. "The wind is powerful cold right now." He spoke with an Irish accent. After handing them each an inflated life vest, he untied the boat from the dock, pulled the rope on board, and neatly wound it up before looping it over a hook. His movements appeared relaxed and unhurried, but he was finished quickly, back behind the wheel, and they were soon on their way.

Nicole held up the vest to see how to put it on. It was a minimal design that reached only to the waist. It had two inflated straps in front meant to keep her afloat and her head out of the water. These straps attached to a belt to be worn around the midsection. At the shoulder they were joined to a rectangular piece, about ten inches long, that reached around her neck and partway down her back. From there, a narrow strap was attached to the rear center of the belt. The vest looked like a men's size extra-large. When she tried it on, the fit was so loose that the front straps kept slipping off her shoulders. She tried to adjust the belt, but it wouldn't fasten any tighter. She thought of asking for a smaller size, but the hook where the life jackets had been hanging was empty. This would have to do.

"How long 'til we reach Yaroslavl?" Reinhardt said.

"An hour, maybe more in this bloody wind," the man said.

Despite the wind, the water was only slightly choppy. After the anxiety of their wait in the garage, the ride seemed peaceful. They were feeling relaxed when the pilot said, "Some bloke is approaching our stern."

Nicole and Reinhardt looked through the plexiglass window behind them. There was a white speck in the distance, growing larger as they watched.

"Let's get rid of them," Reinhardt said. "Can you go faster?"

The boat jerked forward as the pilot put his foot on the gas. "I can speed up," he said, "but that boat is twice our size. It will have a load more horsepower."

"I don't understand," Nicole said. "It can't be the police. How could they have followed us?"

"You're right. It's probably something else," Reinhardt said. "This route is sometimes used by drug smugglers. Or it might be one of the federation's drug-control boats. They wouldn't be looking for you. Still, with an alert out for your arrest, we can't let them find you."

The larger boat was gaining on them. When it was closer, they could hear its loudspeaker booming something in Russian. Reinhardt translated for Nicole. "They're demanding we stop and let them board. They want to search the boat for drugs. Keep going," he told the pilot.

"They're gaining fast," the pilot said. "No way I can outrun them."

"Well, captain, what would you advise?" Reinhardt said.

"I've got a maneuver I've used before." By now, the pilot had to shout to be heard. "When they get a wee bit closer, I'll make a sudden U-turn. They'll follow, but they have to make a wider arc because they're at least twice our size. They might even need two tries. While they're breaking their hearts over that, I'll make another U-turn, so they'll have to turn around a second time. When we're a distance away, I'll steer as close to shore as I can so you two can jump out and swim for land. You both have flotation devices. Take off your coats so they don't weigh you down, and you should be all right. He looked at Nicole in the rearview mirror. "I reckon you can swim. Yeah?"

She nodded. "Of course."

"Wait," Reinhardt said. "How strong a swimmer are you, Nicole?"

"I can do a dozen laps in a swimming pool. I guess you'd say

I'm a strong swimmer under ideal conditions."

"I'm worried about the current," he said. "We'd best swim in tandem. I'll jump first, grab the ladder, and wait to catch you. You'll ride on my back with your arms around my neck. If you can kick, it will help propel us toward shore. If that's too hard, just wrap your legs around me. Got it?"

She nodded, taking off the vest, then the warm, fur-lined coat, which she was sorry to leave behind. She put the vest back on, still a little worried about its loose fit.

"Brace yourselves," the pilot said. "The water is wicked cold. And don't try to swim against the current. Put your effort into edging toward shore. After you leave, I'll keep going. It's too dark for them to see you jump, so they'll stay on my tail. When I'm a ways on, I'll stop and tell them I couldn't hear their loudspeaker over the roar of my engine. They can search the boat. They won't find any drugs. But I'll have to slip them a bribe to avoid being charged with disobeying police orders. A bit of the green usually works with these Russians."

Meanwhile, the drug enforcement craft, manned by three figures, had stopped and was making its turn. As predicted, it couldn't complete the maneuver in a single rotation. It was starting to back up to complete the turn when the speedboat passed and continued on a bit before turning to resume its original direction. They passed drug enforcement for a second time just as it completed its first turn. Now it would have to turn again.

The speedboat continued on until it passed a bend in the river. Here the boat slowed and pulled closer to the shore. Reinhardt got up and moved to the deck's edge. Nicole was right behind him. He put an arm around her and pulled her close. "It looks frightening, but it's going to be all right," he murmured into her hair. "I'll be there to catch you."

Abruptly, he let go and turned to dive into the water. A moment later, he reappeared, holding onto the ladder on the boat's side, waiting for her. Looking at the dark water, Nicole was overcome with a sudden terror, a certainty that—despite Reinhardt's reassurances—this was not going to be all right. Ignoring her instincts, she closed her eyes and forced herself to jump.

When she hit the water, the cold was an overwhelming shock. But what she hadn't anticipated was the force of the current that immediately started pulling her away from Reinhardt and the side of the boat. He managed to grab her flotation vest, but the water was stronger. The vest, loose to begin with, completely slipped off and remained in Reinhardt's hands while Nicole was swept away. She tried to swim, but the current was too swift, and she started to sink. She held her breath as long as she could, hoping Reinhardt would be able to grab her and bring her to the surface. But in the dark, opaque water it was impossible to see. How would he ever find her?

When her breath gave out, she gasped, swallowing water and taking in more through her nose. She choked and gagged, fighting desperately to swim to the surface. From somewhere came a question, *Is this how it ends?* She felt no emotion about it one way or the other. She was too busy fighting the river and the growing need to take a breath.

All at once, Reinhardt grabbed her arm and pulled her to the surface. For a long moment, she fought him, too overcome with coughing and choking to realize she'd been rescued. "It's me," he said. "You're OK. I've got you. Try to calm down so I can get you to shore."

Against every instinct, she managed to stop struggling. He had one arm around her, treading water. "It isn't far to the river's edge," he said. "But I need two arms to get there. Grab me around the neck, and I'll let go of you."

When they reached the shore, he half lifted, half pushed her onto the muddy river bank before climbing out himself.

Still choking, struggling to catch her breath, she felt as if she'd swallowed half the Volga. Reinhardt picked her up and carried her away from the river into the shelter of some trees before putting her down. He pulled her head to one side so she could cough up some of the water she'd swallowed. When her choking stopped, she was left with paroxysms of coughing, which made her chest hurt. A wheezing sound accompanied each labored breath. Her arms and legs were numb with cold, and she was shaking so hard her teeth chattered.

Reinhardt lifted her again and carried her uphill to a road devoid of traffic. He lowered her to the ground next to a tree and propped her against it. "I think it will be easier for you to breathe sitting up," he said.

He pulled out his phone to make a call, then looked at it. "Bloody hell," he said. "The mobile is out of range. I'm going to walk around a bit to get a signal. You're starting to catch your breath, yeah?" He looked at her with concern. "Can you talk?"

She answered with a croaking "Yes," which sent her into another coughing spasm.

"God, I'm sorry," he said. "We should have made that jump together. And the safety vest—I wish I'd checked it out. Right now I'm going to call for help so we can get you somewhere warm and dry."

Nicole was shaking with cold. From her resting place, she watched him walk first in one direction then the other, clearly without any luck. When he stopped back to check on her, he said, "Now the mobile's bloody battery is giving out."

All at once, headlights appeared in the distance. Reinhardt helped Nicole up, and they retreated into the shadow of the trees. The car pulled over to the side, and the driver flashed the headlights off and on.

"That signal's for us." Reinhardt took Nicole's hand and started toward the car.

She pulled away. "How do you know?" she croaked, pausing between words to catch her breath. "Flashing headlights could mean anything."

"No," he said. "It's a signal we use. The chap in the boat said he was going to call in our approximate location. Whoever's in the car probably used thermal imaging to locate us." He grabbed her hand again and pulled her along. "We've got to get you out of the cold."

As they got in, the driver said, "You'll find some blankets back there. Take off your wet things and wrap yourselves in the blankets."

"We can't go to the airport without dry clothes," Reinhardt said. "And my friend here needs to see a doctor first. She almost drowned. You know how polluted the Volga is. At the least, she needs an antibiotic. We'll have to delay the flight until tomorrow."

Nicole undressed under the blanket, leaving her things on the car floor. Reinhardt did the same. Even when she was free of the wet clothes and wrapped in two blankets, she continued to shake with cold. She leaned against Reinhardt, who was also bundled up, but he was just as cold as she was.

They stopped at a tiny, deserted-looking house along a desolate stretch of the road. Inside, it was cold and musty. The driver pulled down the shades and turned on a lamp before using crumpled newspapers to light a log in the fireplace. For the first time, Nicole got a good look at him. He was in his mid-twenties, tall and fit, with curly dark hair pulled back in a ponytail and dark brown eyes. He had regular features, but his strong jawline, prominent forehead, and two-day stubble made him look tough, like someone you wouldn't want to tangle with.

When he caught her looking at him, he held out his hand to shake hers. "The name's Liam. And you are?"

"Nicole," she said. Introductions made, he and Reinhardt started talking. Meanwhile, Nicole took in their surroundings.

The house, a single room, resembled Olga's apartment with rugs on the floor and walls. Liam went to a closet and found them each dry clothes to wear. He also produced a cable to charge Reinhardt's phone. When he was busy connecting it, Nicole went into the bathroom to change. First, she sat in the tub and did her best to wash off the filth from the river. But the tub's spray attachment only emitted a dribble of cold water, and she had no soap. She dried herself on a thin, woven towel before putting on the clothes she'd been given: mustard-color woolen leggings, a well-worn Irish fisherman's sweater, a limp jersey miniskirt, and a faded green cardigan. The leggings fit snuggly, and the fisherman's sweater looked as if it had been shrunk. The sleeves were short, and it didn't completely cover her midriff. Both the tights and sweater were a bit itchy, but at least they were clean and dry. She viewed herself in the mirror and felt ridiculous, unable to decide if she looked sillier with the miniskirt or without it.

When she came out, Reinhardt gave a little laugh and whistled at her. "Cut it out," she said, quickly buttoning up the cardigan to cover her bare middle. She sat on the couch with a blanket wrapped around her to enjoy the fire, while Reinhardt went in to change. He came out dressed in a workman's tan jumpsuit, a radical departure from his usual style. This time it was Nicole's turn to laugh, even though it set off another coughing fit.

Liam left to get a doctor. Reinhardt was busy in the corner that served as a kitchenette. He located a jar of instant coffee and an electric kettle, then pulled a bottle of brandy out of the cupboard. When the coffee was ready, he spiked it with brandy and brought it to Nicole, who was sitting as close to the fire as she dared. Sipping the hot beverage with the mug warming her hands, she began to feel a bit better.

After a while, Liam was back with a doctor, a gray-haired, bearded little man carrying a black satchel. The doctor and Reinhardt carried on a conversation in Russian, presumably about Nicole's near drowning. Liam turned to Nicole and said he was leaving again to pick up something for them to eat. "Do you have any preference?"

"Soup," she gasped. "Hot soup." Each word came out with a wheeze.

"I'll try, but no promises," he said. "It depends on what's open at this hour."

The doctor examined Nicole, listening closely to her chest, then used an instrument to look up her nose and in her ears. Once he was done, he spoke to Reinhardt in Russian, apparently explaining what he'd found. While the doctor was digging in his bag, Reinhardt translated for Nicole. "He says you don't look too bad. You may have aspirated a little water in your lungs but not enough to be alarmed about. He's going to give you a shot of penicillin and a bottle of pills you're to take for a week, mainly because of the polluted water. He says you shouldn't fly for forty-eight hours. But given that you're the object of a manhunt, we need to leave as soon as possible.

"Right now," he went on, "I'm going to make a call to find out the status of our plane. If it's left, I'll ask for it to return tomorrow afternoon. We'll need time in the morning to get new gear and make ourselves presentable. You'll need to work on your disguise again since the Volga washed it away." While he made his call, the doctor proceeded to give Nicole her shot and hand her the bottle of pills. He sat on the couch to wait for the driver to return. Reinhardt joined him, and the two men chatted companionably in Russian over glasses of brandy while Nicole half dozed on the hearth.

It was about an hour before Liam returned, carrying a large bucket marked KFC accompanied by a jumbo-size bag of fries, which the Russian franchise offered instead of the traditional biscuits, mashed potatoes, and gravy served back home. After the delivery, Liam left again to take the doctor home, promising to be back in the morning with the things they needed. Reinhardt had already given him Nicole's passport so it could be copied to give her yet another new identity, one that would give her better cover.

When they were gone, Reinhardt placed the food on the small, wobbly table in the kitchenette corner of the house, and the two of them settled in to eat. It had been fourteen hours since their last meal. Reinhardt seemed to be hungry, but Nicole felt nauseous from all the dirty water she'd swallowed. The thought of the raw sewage and industrial waste in the Volga was enough to make her feel sick.

Nevertheless, she decided to give the food a try. If nothing else, it might get rid of the bad taste in her mouth. She picked up a drumstick, but the Colonel's secret recipe triggered another coughing fit, and she put it down. Reinhardt got up and poured her a tumbler of brandy. She nursed it while she watched him eat, grateful she wasn't hungry.

When they retired, Reinhardt lay on the floor in front of the fireplace, while she spent several miserable hours on the couch coughing. She finally sat up, which eased her chest. She spent the rest of the night in a sitting position, half dozing and wondering if—after so many delays—she was really going home. It hardly seemed possible.

CHAPTER FOURTEEN

REINHARDT'S PHONE WOKE THEM. He answered and muttered a few words before going silent as the other party spoke. When he hung up, he said, "The police have intensified their search for you. They're going door to door in areas surrounding airports within driving distance of Moscow. That includes our airport, Yaroslavl, which isn't far away. Liam is on his way back. He managed to get us some presentable clothes. He also has a new passport, ID, and disguise for you. This time you'll be posing as an old woman."

"Perfect," she said. "These weeks in Russia have aged me at least fifty years. And, after watching Olga, I know just how to play the part."

Reinhardt had put the leftover fried chicken outside for the night to keep it cold. Their tiny refrigerator turned out to be an old-fashioned ice box, which was useless to them since they didn't have the requisite chunk of ice to keep it cold.

He brought the chicken in and offered some to Nicole, but her stomach still felt queasy. She settled for a cup of coffee, while Reinhardt went at the leftovers like a starving man.

Afterward they sat on the couch in front of the fire, Nicole's head resting on Reinhardt's shoulder while she half dozed. They had no idea when Liam would show up. The day ahead was filled with too many worrisome unknowns.

"I'll bet the police's renewed efforts to find you have to do with Kolkov," Reinhardt said. "By now, they'd have noticed he's missing, and they knew he was searching for you. Didn't he say he'd been ordered to find you and bring you in or he'd lose his job?"

She nodded. "His superiors regarded my escape as a dereliction of duty on his part. He'd been humiliated, and he blamed me. He said he was going to kill me to be sure I wouldn't escape this time. You know, I've been thinking about Abby, the reporter who found me sanctuary with Olga. She saved my life. I promised her an exclusive interview about how I'd become a fugitive. I said I'd get in touch with her after I got out of Russia."

"Um-hm," Reinhardt sounded drowsy.

"Are you listening?"

He turned to look at her. "Of course."

"Here's my question. What should I tell her? I certainly can't mention my role as an observer for MI6."

"That's easy," he said. "Just make yourself an innocent bystander, someone persecuted by the Russian police because you were at the scene and made a convenient scapegoat. Obviously, you have to leave out the facts that you actually witnessed the murder and were put on the ship to observe the dissidents. And you'll have to invent a story about how you got out of Russia. Maybe you can tell her you hired the Russian equivalent of a mule, who snuck you out by boat. If she wants more details, explain that you can't be too specific without getting someone in trouble. What you can tell her will make a cautionary tale about traveling abroad, particularly to totalitarian countries. Things like this happen every day to ordinary Russian citizens, although tourists are usually spared because the government wants to encourage them to bring money into the country."

"You're right. That makes a good enough story. Now all I have to do is figure out how to get in touch with her. Her card was in my purse, which I left at Olga's."

He nodded. "Knowing you, I'm sure you'll figure it out."

NANCY BOYARSKY

At that point the conversation turned to their plans for the future once they finally got out of Russia. "First, we'll need to stop in London so I can pack," Reinhardt said. "And I have to make arrangements for storing my furniture and leasing out my flat."

"Oh, Reinhardt," Nicole said. "I'm so worn out! I just want to go home." Her cough was a little better, although she had to stop talking once in a while to catch her breath. "It will take weeks to make those arrangements. You could easily take care of it online once we're back in L.A."

"I don't blame you for wanting to go home," he said. "That's the best place for you to recover after all you've been through. What about this? After we land in Helsinki, you catch a flight home. I'll go to London. Then, once I get things sorted out—"

She pulled out of his arms and stared at him. "Are you kidding? Last time we had that arrangement, I didn't see you again for all those months. If you really have to stop in London, I'm coming with you. In fact, I'm not letting you out of my sight until we're in L.A."

"But you said you were too tired to stop in London."

"I'd feel a lot worse worrying about what had become of you if you disappeared again."

"That's not going to happen, Nicole. I've given you my word." He was silent a while before going on. "But I do understand why you might worry, even though it's unnecessary. What about this? We'll stop at my digs for a couple of days while I pack what I need and make some basic arrangements for my flat. That way you'll have time to rest between flights."

Torn between her desire to go home and her fear of letting Reinhardt wander off on his own, she agreed.

By noon, there was still no sign of Liam, and they were growing anxious. What if the police arrived before he did? They sat down to lunch with a greatly depleted bottle of brandy and the KFC bucket between them. Only a half dozen pieces were left. Nicole

196

took one. After removing the now-soggy crust with the spicy seasoning, she was able to get some chicken down, following each bite with a sip of brandy to ease her cough.

They were just finishing up when a knock at the door brought them to their feet. Reinhardt went over to the window and moved the shade slightly so he could peek out. He immediately opened the door. It took Nicole a moment to recognize the man who walked in. Liam had changed from the pea coat and khakis he'd been wearing earlier to a black padded jacket with black pants and heavy workman's boots. Topping it off was an odd hat with a narrow brim in front that ended with earflaps long enough to reach his collar. Following close behind him was an enormous tan dog with a black muzzle and sad eyes. Liam passed several packages to Reinhardt before turning to usher in the dog—which had been hovering uncertainly in the doorway—and lock the door.

"In the packages are new coats and clothes for you both and the kit you requested to turn Nicole into an old woman. I saw a patrol car in front of a house about ten kilometers down the road. There are about three or four places they'll probably search before they get here." He paused to look down at his boots and pat the front of his jacket. "In case you didn't notice, I'm dressed as a laborer. I'll tell the police I'm staying here temporarily. The dog is Borya. He's a Mastiff, one of Russians' favorite breeds. I borrowed him, reckoning he'd make me look more authentic. Here's my story: This house belonged to my dear old granny, who passed a month ago. I'm here to sort the place out so I can sell it. Now let's get you into hiding." He handed them the packages he'd brought before leading them to a corner of the house and pulling aside one of the rugs.

Beneath it was a worn wooden floor marked with many blemishes, knot holes, and, in one spot, a large burn mark. "Stand back," he said, before giving the burn mark a thump with his fist.

A trap door, undetectable until that moment, silently sprung upward. It worked like a kitchen cupboard set to open with a push instead of a pull. Nicole and Reinhardt walked over to look down. A ladder led into darkness. Liam reached under a floorboard and clicked a button that lit up a good-sized room below.

"Best go down now. We don't know how soon the police will get here. The room has a vent to the outside, so you don't have to worry about running out of air. But remember not to talk or make any noise once the police get here. You'll hear them arrive, and they'll be able to hear you."

"What about my cough?"

"Brandy!" Both Reinhardt and Liam replied in unison. Liam went on. "You'll find a bottle down there. Don't stint on it. Get blotto if that's what it takes."

Reinhardt went down first, followed by Nicole. The basement room was much nicer than the one above, clean and bright with a small, modern kitchen. It had a real refrigerator, a microwave, and a toaster oven. The cupboard was stocked with food: several varieties of crackers; shelf-stable milk; cereal; jars of peanut butter, marmite, and processed cheese spread; as well as cans of soup and tuna. A bottle of vodka and another of Reinhardt's beloved brandy sat on the counter. He opened the brandy, poured two glasses, and handed one to Nicole. "Remember what Liam said. Small sips to soothe your throat. Best start in."

He sat down at a desk equipped with a computer and turned it on. Apparently, the basement had Wi-Fi because he was able to find a Russian paper and was soon engrossed in it.

She looked around the room. It was well fitted out. They could survive down here for days, maybe even weeks. Aside from the food, computer, and Wi-Fi, there was a tiled bathroom with a real shower. Nicole was dying to use it, but she had to wait until the cops came, searched the place, and left.

Before too long, there was a knock at the door above and

198

murmurs of conversation. Nicole couldn't make out the words, but she could tell they were speaking Russian. From what she could hear, their tone seemed low-key enough to assure her they bought Liam's story about his grandmother's death.

After five minutes or so, the footsteps stopped, and Nicole realized they all must have sat down. She could picture Liam, playing host by offering them some vodka, which they'd be unable to resist. Meanwhile, she silently began to empty the contents of the bags Liam had brought. She took out the overcoats and hung them on a hook. Both were black and made of heavy wool, practically identical except for size. The second bag contained shoes, socks, slacks, boxer shorts, a shirt, and a jacket for Reinhardt.

The last bag held a black dress that looked as if it would be too big and too long, thermal underwear, thick, opaque flesh-colored tights, and a pair of black, low-heeled, lace-up shoes like old women used to wear in her great grandmother's day. At the bottom of the bag was a box containing makeup, a packet of tissues, several eyeliner pencils, a palette of eye shadow, a bottle of rubber cement, another of nail polish remover, and a short white wig. Whoever packed it had included a hand mirror and several pages of instructions explaining how to apply the makeup. Only when Nicole picked it up and saw herself in the mirror did she realize how awful she looked. Her hair was stiff and sticking out on one side. Her face had a brownish cast from the dirty river, which her soapless wash in cold water had failed to remove. She'd have to take a shower before working on her makeup.

At last they heard footsteps heading toward the door and an exchange that sounded like a friendly parting. The place was silent for only a few minutes before the knocking resumed. A brief conversation ensued with more of an edge to it than before, then the sound of boots walking through the house. The dog started barking. Liam shouted at him, and he stopped.

Nicole could tell they'd rolled back the rugs by the clatter of their boots on the bare floor. Apparently, they'd been so taken in by Liam's hospitality that they'd neglected to look for a basement or other possible hiding places. As they walked around, they tapped on the floor, apparently looking for a sign there might be empty space under the house. Whoever had fitted out the basement room had provided some way of disguising the echo from the hollow space below. After a while, the rugs were put back, softening the sound of them walking back to the door. They left, and everything was quiet. But Reinhardt and Nicole decided to stay where they were for a while in case the men returned yet again. Nicole lay down on the couch. Still exhausted from her bad night, she fell asleep for a few minutes, only to wake when the trap door opened.

"It's safe to come up now," Liam said. "They're really gone this time."

"Can I stay down here and use the shower?" Nicole said.

"Of course. I'll be driving you to the airport as soon as I confirm your plane is ready for boarding. You can wait down there if you want. It might be more comfortable. We were limited in what we could do upstairs. It had to look authentic. But our engineers did more with the basement in case someone had to stay longer than a day or two.

Nicole took her time in the shower, adjusting the temperature to the hottest she could stand, enjoying the luxury of having not just soap but also shampoo and conditioner. When she was done, she put on the clothes Liam had brought. As expected, the black dress was long and baggy, a perfect combination with the lace-up, orthopedic shoes for the role she'd be playing.

She felt refreshed by the shower, even though she was still coughing and a little sluggish from the brandy. She sat down at a small table in the corner and read the instructions from the makeup box. It explained how to apply the products to add decades to her appearance. The sheet had been downloaded from the web. It appeared to be written for actors or makeup artists.

Applying rubber cement to her face seemed to be the key, followed up by gently pinching her skin until the cement dried, creating creases and wrinkles. She needed another pair of hands to help with this, so she enlisted Reinhardt. He pretended to be repelled by what was happening to her face but gave himself away by laughing. "You don't look that bad, really. Just a lot older. I do hope the rubber cement doesn't pull out your eyebrows when you take it off."

Nicole hadn't thought of that. But after rereading the instructions, she was reassured. The adhesive was supposed to come off easily with soap and water. For more stubborn areas, nail polish remover had been included in the kit. Whoever packed it had been thorough. She used an eyeliner pencil to add lines and crow's feet to her wrinkled face, then applied blue eye shadow under her eyes to create bags. Next came the white wig. In some areas, fake scalp showed through, making it look like the thinning hair of the very old.

When Nicole saw herself in the mirror, she was startled by the person looking back at her. The wig and makeup kit had done a good job. She looked ancient. She carried their new coats upstairs, where Reinhardt and Liam were waiting.

"I'm ready to leave," she said.

Both men stared at her. "Mother of God!" Liam murmured, while Reinhardt just smiled and shook his head at her transformation. Liam handed Nicole a passport with a photo of an old woman and a Russian ID card with the same picture. Studying it, Nicole could see that it really did look like her, only much, much older. Graphic software must have been used to age her image on her fake passport. The app's tools had dramatically changed her appearance in much the same way the makeup kit had.

NANCY BOYARSKY

As they left the house, Liam said, "I have baggage for both of you in the boot. They're packed with clothes consistent with your disguises. I also have a written directive that should allow me to drive you directly to the plane. If all goes according to plan, you won't be subjected to a search or even asked to present ID."

At long last they were heading for the airport. Several patrol cars, sirens blaring, passed them on the road, forcing them to pull over while they went by. Nicole wondered where they were going and why. But this wasn't her worry. She'd soon be in the air, on her way out of Russia.

They turned onto the airport access road and immediately had to stop. A major traffic jam was up ahead. The police appeared to be stopping and searching every car before admitting it to the airport's main approach.

"Shouldn't we turn around and try again later?" Nicole said.

"No," both Reinhardt and Liam said at the same time. Reinhardt finished the thought. "A U-turn will only make them suspicious and trigger a chase. We'd hoped we wouldn't run into something like this, but we're well prepared. You're going to lie down and pretend you're a very sick woman. That's our cover. You have a serious illness, and we're going to Helsinki, where they have advanced treatments for it."

By the time they reached the head of the line, Reinhardt was in the front seat with Liam. Nicole was lying in back pretending to be asleep.

A policeman came over and opened the driver's door. He gave an abrupt command, ordering them out of the car. Liam and Reinhardt climbed out and, at the cop's request, showed their IDs. Meanwhile, two other uniformed officers pulled open the trunk, took out the suitcases, and began to search them.

The policeman who'd ordered Reinhardt and Liam out opened the back door. Reinhardt stepped forward and, after handing over Nicole's ID, delivered a description of the malady she was

202

supposed to be suffering from. The cop gave a sharp retort. His attitude seemed to be that even a sick old woman wouldn't be allowed past without getting out of the car and presenting her own ID.

Turning away from Reinhardt, the officer stuck his head in and shined a flashlight in Nicole's face. It didn't take much to bring on a coughing fit, and she was now in the middle of one. When she stopped and caught her breath, she moaned. She must have looked truly dreadful, for the man stepped away and quietly closed the door. When he spoke to Reinhardt again, his voice had lost the hostile tone, and he threw in the word "babushka" several times.

The policeman waved Liam and Reinhardt back in the car and directed them to park on the opposite side of the road, which was empty of traffic. Once they'd reparked, Reinhardt said, "We're OK. Nicole, you were brilliant! They're sending for a car to escort us to our plane." When it arrived, two officers got out and Liam and Reinhardt had to show their IDs again, as well as Nicole's.

At last the cops got back in their car and beckoned Liam to follow. They drove around the perimeter of the airfield where a small plane was waiting. "They've rented you a Cessna Citation." Liam's voice was filled with admiration. "They'll be bringing something to carry Nicole onto the plane, a stretcher or a collapsible wheelchair."

It turned out to be a wheelchair. A couple of tough-looking workmen rolled it onto the tarmac. Nicole moaned and went limp as the pair, obviously inexperienced at this particular task, lifted her out of the car and onto the wheelchair. They gently carried it up the stairs and into the plane, placing Nicole and the chair in the middle of the cabin before securing the brakes. Nicole slouched and drooped her head forward, as if it was difficult for her to hold herself upright.

As they left, one of the men said something to her that ended with *matushka*, a word she knew meant *mother*. She regarded this with some amusement since they were at least twenty years her senior. She had to assume these men had mothers they cared about and were wishing her good luck. She gave a slight smile of acknowledgement along with a nod before drooping her head again, as if the effort had been too much.

The plane's engine had begun to warm up when the pilot's voice came on the loudspeaker. "The control tower has ordered us to stop. Some higher-up has told the police to board the plane and make sure we aren't hiding a fugitive. Buckle up! We're lifting off."

Nicole dashed from the wheelchair into the seat next to Reinhardt. She'd just fastened her seatbelt when the plane went aloft and began gaining altitude with incredible speed. Below, four police cars drove onto the runway, too late to catch up with the plane. Cops piled out, each holding an automatic weapon, but the plane was safely out of range. Just then another vehicle came around the nearest building. It was a heavy truck with a large metal compartment on top.

"Bloody hell," Reinhardt breathed when he saw it. "They've brought in a rocket launcher. That thing can blow us out of the sky."

The men on the ground were shrinking as the plane tilted steeply upward. The wheelchair, its brakes still locked, slid to the back of the plane and crashed against the bathroom door. From below, they heard a boom. Looking past Reinhardt who was in the window seat, Nicole could see a puff of smoke. After a moment, a projectile was heading toward them. The plane suddenly swerved from its path, making Nicole and the others tilt sharply to one side.

The missile sailed by, several hundred feet from their window. As they watched, it blew up in midair. The force of the explosion made the plane jerk sideways, then suddenly drop before resuming its ascent.

Nicole closed her eyes and buried her face in Reinhardt's shoulder. He put his arms around her and held her. When the plane had steadied itself, he said, "We're safe. We're well out of their range now."

There was a long silence as the plane climbed ever higher. The pilot came back on the speaker. "You folks may not realize how lucky you are to be flying in this model Cessna. It's the fastest climbing aircraft in the world. In any other plane, our chances of getting out of Yaroslavl alive would have been nil. I'm leveling off now at forty-one thousand feet. You can release your seatbelts and move around the cabin. We'll be in Helsinki in about an hour and forty minutes."

Nicole undid her seatbelt and went into the bathroom to remove the wig and wash off the rubber cement holding the wrinkles in place. She pulled her hair into a ponytail. She didn't look too bad. Her face was mottled with red in places, but at least she could recognize herself.

The steward brought out drinks, then a substantial meal of prime rib and Yorkshire pudding. Feeling sleepy after the big meal, Nicole cuddled up to Reinhardt. She felt safe and comforted by his closeness, the faint smell of aftershave that clung to him, and his own unique scent, which was part of the reason she found him so irresistible.

Once again, she wondered what the future held for them. Would he be satisfied with his new life in L.A. as a settled family man? Or would the siren call of MI6 be too much for him to resist if—no, *when*—they reached out to him again? She wondered, too, how much time would have to pass before she could stop worrying about it.

He leaned toward her and whispered, "Are you asleep?"

"No. I'm just trying to relax after our narrow escape. Talk to me. Tell me something about yourself I don't know."

"You already know everything."

"Not really. You've never talked about your life before we met. I know you were a DCI with the London police. But what about your family, your upbringing? You've never said anything about your life growing up. Who were your parents? What were they like? How and why did you ever become a spy? Is that what you always wanted to do?"

"Whoa," he said. "Too many questions. It will take me the rest of the trip to answer them."

"I don't have anything better to do," she said.

He smiled. "All right, but stop me when I start to bore you."

"That's not going to happen."

"My parents divorced when I was five," he said. "I have little memory of my father. You see, he was a spy for the British intelligence services. My mother left him for the same reason you'd leave me if I ever went back to MI6. She couldn't stand the sudden, unexplained absences, the risks she knew he was taking. He came to see me a few times between assignments, but I was too young to form any real memory of him. We had a few photos around the house, and I used to study them. They didn't reveal anything about what kind of man he was or what it would have been like to spend time with him.

"My mother was a wonderful woman. I adored her. But, in accord with family tradition, I was sent off to boarding school when I was seven. Shortly after that, my father was killed on an assignment. I never did learn the details. Just that he was regarded as some kind of hero by the branch of British intelligence that later became MI6. His picture is on the wall at headquarters with other operatives who died in the line of duty. After that, my mother remarried. I never got on with my stepfather, and they travelled a lot. So I usually spent holidays with the families of my mates from school."

She'd been leaning against his shoulder. Now she pulled away and looked at him. He was gazing out the window, but he didn't appear sad revisiting these old memories. "How terrible for you," she said.

"Not really. I didn't know what it was like to have a close family. And there were other boys in similar situations. I accepted this as the norm. The ones with happy families were the exception. How am I doing? Bored yet?"

"No, go on. Tell me about how you became a spy—even after your father's profession brought about your parent's divorce and his death." She leaned against him again, and he put his arm around her.

"I joined the police force first, as you know. I was always attracted to law enforcement, perhaps because of my father. Then, a couple of years ago, MI6 recruited me after I was involved in several well-publicized cases. I think they were interested once they realized I was the son of one of their heroes. I didn't give the decision much thought. The work was exciting, and there wasn't time for self-reflection. That is, until we broke up, and I thought I'd lost you to Jonah—"

"Josh," she interrupted. She wondered if he always got Josh's name wrong to tease her or if he was jealous because she'd almost married Josh after she and Reinhardt broke up.

"Josh," he corrected himself. "That's when I realized how much I wanted to marry you and for the two of us to build the family I never had." He gave a laugh. "Now I'm sounding like one of those modern love stories from the newspaper."

He pointed out the window. "Look." They'd just emerged from the cloud cover into a different world, where the sky was blue and the sun shining.

"We did it," he said. "We got away. Shall we have the steward bring us a bottle of brandy?"

"Brandy? Hell, no," Nicole said. "This calls for a real celebration! We're on our way home." She turned to call out to the steward, "Can you please bring us a bottle of champagne?"

ACKNOWLEDGEMENTS

MY FIRST THANKS GO TO MY HUSBAND, Bill, who (as always) read every draft of this book and helped me shape the plot and characters. A special thanks to fellow author Dave Edlund for reading an early draft and providing great suggestions on how to approach an international thriller. Thanks also to my early readers, my sister Susan Scott and Cathy Watkins, who gave me ideas and caught plot glitches. And, of course, thanks to my family, Jennifer, John, Anabelle, and Lila, who looked after us and kept us sane during the terrible year of the pandemic.

ABOUT THE AUTHOR

NANCY BOYARSKY IS THE AWARD-WINNING AUTHOR of the *Nicole Graves Mysteries*. Her books have been compared to the work of Mary Higgins Clark and Sue Grafton. They've also been praised for contributing to the "women-driven mystery field with panache" (*Foreword Reviews*) and their "hold-onto-the-bar roller coaster" plots (*RT Book Reviews*).

Nancy coauthored *Backroom Politics*, a *New York Times* notable book, with her husband Bill Boyarsky. She has contributed to several political anthologies and written for publications such as the *Los Angeles Times*, *The California Journal*, and *Forbes*. She was communications director for political affairs for ARCO. Her debut novel, *The Swap*—book one of the *Nicole Graves Mysteries*—won the prestigious Eric Hoffer Award for Best Micro Press Book of the Year. In addition to writing mysteries, Nancy is producer and director of the podcast *Inside California Politics*.

THE NICOLE GRAVES SERIES

BY NANCY BOYARSKY

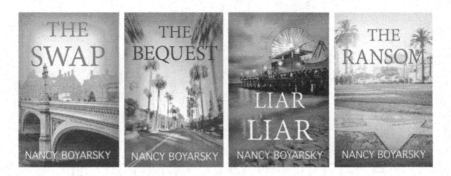

"Nicole Graves is the best fictional sleuth
to come down the pike since Sue Grafton's Kinsey Millhone."
–Laura Levine, author of the popular *Jaine Austen Mysteries*

"Nicole Graves is a charming and straight-shooting heroine"
–*Foreword Reviews*

"Boyarsky's weightless complications expertly combine menace
with bling, making the heroine's adventures both nightmarish
and dreamy."
–*Kirkus Reviews*

"*Liar Liar* creates exquisite tension…"–*Midwest Book Review*